Secret Visions

Pat O'Connor

Every truth passes through three stages before it is recognized. In the first, it is ridiculed. In the second, it is opposed. In the third, it is regarded as self-evident.

Arthur Schopenhauer 1788 - 1860

Chapter 1

The gray skies blackened the turquoise water, and the air sizzled with pent-up tension as Annie Mc-Doogan floated in the warm South Florida current. The impending storm mirrored her mood, and she felt strangely empowered. It was a perfect beach day.

Annie had been deeply depressed since someone killed her father six months ago. They had been very close, and she cried every night now that he was gone. Her mother, Colleen, had sold their house and moved them 12 miles west to Coral Springs because the Fort Lauderdale memories were too much for her to handle. She agreed to homeschool Annie until she felt strong enough to attend classes. The ocean was Annie's only joy now, and her mother brought her as often as possible.

The beach was almost deserted. It was the last Monday in April, and the other kids were still in school. Annie, her mom and a lifeguard had the sand to themselves. Just the way Annie liked it. She had gained 20 pounds since her father died, and the fewer people who saw her in a bathing suit, the better.

Her mood improved as the wind picked up, and she playfully conquered the crashing waves. Her white swimsuit made her an easy target to spot in the dark water, and she knew her mother would yell at her if she drifted too far in any direction.

She marveled as schools of fish leaped in the distance while the circling gulls feasted. *Wait a minute. That's not right. Something's off.*

"Annie! Annie! Get out!"

She glanced back at the beach and saw her mother frantically waving her arms. *What's wrong?*

Time slowed down as her brain registered everything that was going on. *Mother upset. Fish getting closer.* She suddenly felt like an actor in a movie, paralyzed as she watched the scene unfold. *This can't be real.*

So many birds. So many fish. Surrounding her now, rubbing against her. *This isn't right.* Her heart was pounding harder. She needed to run. *I can't think!*

Out of the corner of her eye, she saw the lifeguard running toward a Jet Ski 100 yards down the beach. *Another actor in the story. Not enough time.* She could hear the faint sound of sirens wailing in the distance. *Coming for me?*

Focus, Annie, focus. Breathe. You know what's happening.

"Daddy!" The wind whipped her words away.

She felt movement. *There it is!* A black fin, moving faster and faster. Coming straight at her. Emotionless. Relentless. On target.

I'm hit! Instant clarity. *No damage!* Annie searched for her attacker in the black water. *Where are you?* Her heart was about to explode. *Somebody help me!*

The outside world fell silent. No birds or screams. No help. No sirens. Just her and the unseen shark alone in a bubble. *I can't run. My legs won't move!*

Her entire focus centered on the water around her. Crouching now, she waited. Every nerve firing as her muscles tensed for action. *Come on. I'm only 15, and I'm not going to die here.* She breathed deeply and steadied her body. Waiting.

The wind died. *Fin!* Slowly circling her. Annie instinctively matched its movements, turn for turn, finally able to move her legs. *Should I run? If I fall, I'm dead. I don't know what to do!* The words screamed in her head, and she could hear her blood pounding.

Breathe.

Whoosh! Teeth clamped on her leg as she stared into dark, malevolent eyes.

Remember what I taught you.

She twisted and turned but couldn't pull away. The shark was motionless while it tasted the raw flesh, sampling her like an appetizer. The bloody water fueled her rage, boiling inside her and pushing her to act. Giving her strength. Fear disappeared. She was the hunter now. *This isn't over.*

Annie tensed as she pulled back her hand and jabbed her finger in the cold, hard eye. Teeth sank deeper into her leg. *Damn it!*

She channeled her anger and smashed her fist into the killer's gills. *Bam!* The stunned shark released its grip and thrashed its tail, forcing her under the crimson water. *I'm down. I can't fight.*

Annie didn't know when the seizures started or when she lost consciousness. But, her mother knew. Colleen could see Annie floating face down in the water with her arms stretched out at her sides like a bloody snow angel. She screamed in anguish as she watched her daughter drift away.

Chapter 2

Annie felt no pain as she looked down at her body laid out on the sand. Watching the man crouched over her, pushing on her chest. *Looks bad.* She felt no connection to the empty shell below her.

The tunnel was dark and somewhat foreboding, but peace surrounded her as she emerged and floated upward toward the bright golden light. An indescribable feeling of ecstasy enveloped her in a soft cloud of unconditional love. She was being touched by untold numbers of beings. Pure love poured over her in waves. *I want to stay here forever.*

Daddy! Her father appeared suddenly beside her, dressed in white and glowing with joy.

Pumpkin. She sensed his words rather than hearing them. He seemed to communicate using pictures. *It's not your time. You have to go back.*

No! I want to stay here with you. I miss you.

Honey, you have to leave. You must make my death mean something. The world has to change, and you will lead the movement. He smiled at his only child. *You can do this.* She felt lost, and found, all at the same time. *How can I change anything? I'm just a kid.*

Use your brain. The ideas will come. You can make the world a better place.

Daddy...

He held his arms wide and started walking backward. *Now, you have to go. Mom's waiting for you.*

Daddy, please don't make me go back! She wanted to stay with him in this wondrous place for eternity.

"Okay, we've got a pulse!" The paramedics sighed with relief. This girl was too special to lose.

"Hello, Miss Annie. You had an accident and are in the Holy Cross Hospital. My name's Tamika, and I'm your nurse while you're in Intensive Care."

"What happened? Where's Daddy?"

"I don't know 'bout your poppa, but your momma's in the cafeteria. She's been sittin' at your bedside all day. You fought off a shark attack. Girl, you're a real hero around here. Reporters are lining up to talk to you. How you feelin'?"

The island lilt in her voice was warm and comforting, and Annie relaxed a little. "My leg hurts. Like it's on fire." Tears rolled slowly down her cheeks.

"That's where the shark got you, baby, but your leg will heal. I'll give you more pain medicine. Your momma will be here when you wake up."

Colleen McDoogan gazed lovingly at her sleeping daughter while she prayed for her quick recovery. The last six months had been hard for both of them. The real estate market was slow, and sales were few and far between. Money was tight, and they were both still drowning in grief.

"Mommy?" Annie slowly opened her eyes.

Colleen took Annie's hand. Tears filled her eyes as she tried to find the words to express her emotion. "Welcome back, pumpkin."

"Pumpkin. Daddy called me that," she said as a frown formed on her freckled face.

"I guess it's been awhile since you've heard it." A slight grimace pulled the corners of her mouth down.

"No, I saw Daddy after the attack. I floated toward a bright light, and he was there. He looked so happy, but he made me come back."

Colleen's heart skipped a beat. "What do you mean?"

"I was in a beautiful place, and I wanted to stay there forever." She had a far away look in her eyes as the memory came flooding back.

"You wanted to die?" Colleen whispered the words.

Annie snapped out of her reverie and started twirling her long red hair around her finger. "I wasn't dead. I was still me, just different. Better."

Colleen got up and sat on the bed, wrapping her arms around Annie as she pressed her lips on her daughter's hair. "Oh, baby. It's just your imagination. We both miss your father." She tried to hold back the sobs, but soon they were crying in each other's arms.

Colleen went back to her chair as an aide delivered the supper tray. "You'll be going home in a couple of days. The doctors want to make sure the wound's not infected before they let you go."

Annie nodded as she picked at her food. Her mom didn't believe her, so she didn't feel like talking anymore. Instead, she focused on building a mashed-potato tower.

"Father Sullivan's making his rounds today. He said that he'd stop by to see you this evening."

Annie groaned. "I don't want to see him. He'll try to find some way to make this my fault. I'll pretend I'm asleep if I hear him coming."

"Oh, Annie, he's worried about you."

Annie tried to sit up straighter in the bed. "Since daddy died, he's started telling me what to do."

Colleen gave her daughter a sad smile. "He was your father's best friend."

"But he's not daddy!"

Colleen dropped the subject and leaned forward in her chair. "The reporters are downstairs. They're offering a lot of money for pictures and a story."

Annie lowered her head and clenched her fingers around the fork as she dug a moat around the tower.

Colleen continued to talk quickly in a low voice. "Insurance doesn't cover all the hospital costs. We need the money to pay the bill."

"No, I don't want to talk about it with strangers. How can you even ask me to let somebody take pictures? My leg is so ugly."

"That doesn't matter. We need the money." She'd been trying to hide their money problems from Annie, but they couldn't afford to turn down this opportunity. Annie erupted in fury. "No! You're not using me. You don't believe anything I told you. You don't care what kind of pictures people want to take. I want to go back with daddy in that beautiful place. I'm not going to help you!"

Colleen knew that any further discussion was pointless until Annie had time to cool off and consider her request. After she said goodbye, Tamika came over to check on her patient. She sat in the chair that Colleen had just vacated and scooted it closer to the bed.

"I hear you talkin' to your momma, and I reckon you think you saw your dead poppa." She brushed the hair out of Annie's eyes and tilted her chin up. "Baby, you had a seizure and drowned. Seizures happen to some people when they get overloaded with emotions. Your heart stopped beating. You was dead, girl. I've been an ICU nurse for 20 years, and I hear lots of stories like yours." She stroked Annie's hair and whispered the words she longed to hear. "I believe you."

Annie shuttered, pulled her good leg up to her chest, dropped her head down and slowly started to rock back and forth. Tamika could barely hear her low moans. After a few minutes, she recovered enough to speak. She looked straight into Tamika's eyes. "I want to go back."

Tamika shook her head. "That's not right. God saved your life for a reason. Don't waste it, child." She patted Annie's hand. "You'll get back there soon enough. No sense rushin' it."

Annie thought about that for a moment and nodded in agreement. "Okay."

"Baby, there's lots of books out there 'bout near-death experiences. Read a few and let your momma read them too. It'll help her understand."

"I'll get some. Thanks, Tamika."

"You welcome, Miss Annie, and I'll give you the phone numbers for a couple of nice kids 'bout your age who went through the same thin' not too long ago. They were patients of mine. Do you good to talk to them." She got up and fluffed the pillows for Annie before she left. "Everythin' will be okay. You'll see."

Except that daddy wants me to change the world.

Chapter 3

The next two days in the hospital dragged slowly by. Annie learned to walk with crutches, and she agreed to let her mother negotiate the publication rights to her story. She was bored and wanted to go home.

However, she wasn't ready for the reporters who were waiting outside the hospital. Everybody wanted her picture, and the flashbulbs temporarily blinded her. She almost tripped over the curb and would have fallen if her mother hadn't caught her. Annie didn't bother to answer the shouted questions since a journalist from a teen magazine was coming to the house next week to interview her. She was dreading it.

The ride home was a quiet one. Annie was in pain and didn't feel like talking. However, when she walked into her bedroom and saw the poster of Michio Kaku hanging over her bed, she smiled for the first time in days. She loved physics, and he was her inspiration. Stephen Hawking looked down from the opposite wall, and a statue of Albert Einstein stood on her dresser. She was a geek and proud of it and hoped that her geekiness would earn her a college scholarship to a good school.

Annie hobbled over to her computer desk, threw her crutches on the bed and started researching the Internet for near-death articles. The computer was her best friend. Literally. No one had called or visited her while she was in the hospital. She was a loner by nature, and homeschooling had made her even more reclusive. She knew it but was unable to change.

At the end of the day, she managed to download a few promising library books and started devouring the stories written by authors who had experienced near-death visions. It seemed that people from all different religions reported similar events but with their own cultural spin. Annie set about to find the common threads in the tales. She had a mission now, and it helped pull her out of her depression. Her mom brought her supper to her room, and she read through the night. Her mind was like a sponge, soaking up everything she could find.

When she woke in the morning, she had the beginnings of a plan of how to fulfill her father's request. But, as much as she hated to admit it, she knew she couldn't do it alone. She rummaged through her purse and found the phone numbers for Ming and Emir that Tamika had given her. She called them that evening, and they were both eager to meet the Shark Girl, who they had heard about on TV. They agreed to come over to her house Monday after school.

The first thing Annie saw through the peephole was spiky blue hair. She flung open the door to the most exotic person that she had ever seen. Cleopatra eye makeup, tattoos, piercings and bohemian clothes completed the picture and made Annie regret wearing her faded T-shirt and baggy pants. The two girls couldn't be more different.

Before a word was spoken, Ming swept into the house like a queen leading her entourage. "Hello, darling. Enjoying your fame?" She leaned over and air-kissed both of Annie's cheeks. "I'm Ming."

Is she for real? "Hi, come on in."

Ming strode around the living room examining the crucifixes on the wall as Annie struggled to keep up with her. "I'm so glad school's almost over. The rains have already started, and it's just the worst thing ever to get caught in a storm. Fabulous house. Could you get me a glass of water? I walked over from school, and it's so hot out there. I'm absolutely dying of thirst."

Will I get her a glass of water? "Can't walk and carry at the same time." She waved a crutch at Ming. "The kitchen's through there and clean glasses are in the dishwasher."

Ming hit her forehead with the palm of her hand. "Oh, I'm the dumbest person in the whole world. Go sit down, and I'll get my own drink."

At that point, the doorbell rang, and Annie noticed a red BMW convertible parked alongside the curb. All she could see through the peephole was a chin. Annie opened the door and suddenly forgot how to speak. Her jaw dropped as she stared up at the Adonis in front of her. Black hair, soulful eyes, tanned skin, broad shoulders and slim hips. The total package. His face cracked open in a brilliant smile, and her crutches started shaking. This guy was beautiful.

Oomph! Ming pushed Annie aside as she rushed in. "Hi Emir, I'm Ming." She stood on her tiptoes and leaned in to kiss his cheek, but Emir instinctively stepped back and raised his hands in front of his chest. Ming had to settle for a high-five. "Nice clothes, man. Is that Beemer outside yours?"

"Yes, I got it a month ago for my 16th birthday. My folks wanted me to get a black one because they think black is the color of success. I told them if they gave me a black one, I'd trade it in for a pickup truck." He grinned at the memory. "I got my red dream girl." He shook his head slightly and lowered his eyes. "I'm the only kid at school with a convertible." He looked uncomfortable as he ran his fingers through his luxurious hair.

Annie led the way into the living room. "Come on in and sit down. I'm still not used to standing. Mom made some sandwiches, and there's fruit if you're hungry."

"Do you have any pasta?" Ming liked a bowl of noodles after school.

"No, sandwiches and fruit. That's it." She plopped down in a chair and rested her leg on the coffee table. She winced as her jeans brushed against the wound.

"Hey, can we see the shark bite?" Emir was genuinely curious.

Annie sighed. "No, it's gross. The shark ripped off a chunk of my thigh." She unconsciously patted her leg like she was checking to see if it was still there.

"Mom promised a magazine that it could take pictures, so photos will be all over the Internet in a couple of weeks." Her eyes welled up with tears as everyone sat in an uncomfortable silence.

"Well, we know about *your* accident, so why don't I tell you about *mine?*" Emir took a bite of his apple as he collected his thoughts and considered how much of the truth he wanted to tell them. "My name's Emir Polat. My parents are from Turkey, and they're both doctors. They want me to be a doctor too, which means I have to ace my exams. Two weeks ago, I was having problems studying for my Advanced Placement Biology test."

Ming moved a little closer to him on the couch and smiled up at him. "It's hard to imagine you having any problems."

He ignored her advances, took another bite of the apple and thought about what to say next. It was all so fresh. "My parents wanted me to do well so that next year I can take AP courses in chemistry and physics. And, they had just given me the new car." He frowned and pulled on his ear while the girls sat mesmerized by his deep voice. "I couldn't focus, so a buddy of mine gave me some pills to help me study, and I overdosed."

The wide-eyed girls stared at him. This guy took drugs?

"Mom popped in to check on me, and I wasn't breathing. She started CPR and dialed 911. And here I am. The docs estimate I was gone for about ten minutes." His palms were sweating as he wiped them on his khakis. "I went on the same kind of trip that everybody reads about. Tunnel, floating, white light and dead relatives. I saw my aunt, but I felt like I was in touch with the Universe. Amazing, freakin' amazing. My parents are still mad at me because the test isn't offered again until next year."

Ming reached over and grabbed some grapes. "I'm sure you'll do great." She started to pat him on his knee, but he moved it out of the way. "I guess I'm next. My name's Ming Chang, and I'm second generation Chinese American. Mom's an artist, and dad's a concert pianist. They're cool and let me be myself. I want to be an actor and plan to move to New York or LA when I graduate in a couple of years."

She paused a moment to give the other two a chance to say how good she would be. When that didn't happen, she frowned slightly before continuing. "A couple of months ago, I was in a car accident. I was on a date with a gorgeous senior. He was driving and lost control of the car. He was killed when we crashed into a telephone pole. I was thrown out of the car, split my head open on a rock and floated over my body, watching the paramedics."

That went too fast for Annie. "Why did he lose control?"

"He swerved to avoid a dog, hit an oil slick, and we crashed." That was what she had told the police, so she might as well tell Annie and Emir the same thing.

Annie still wasn't satisfied. "Why didn't you have your seat belt on?"

Geesh! She wasn't on trial here. "Because I wanted to put my head on his shoulder." She said that too loudly, but at least that part was almost true. "Anyway, that's about it. No pain. Just this wonderful feeling of being whole and part of something great. I wanted to stay. I was so happy when I started floating up, but then I dropped back down. I never saw anybody. Out of all the books I've read, it looks like I'm one of the few who never had an encounter. It's just not fair!" Her lower lip jutted out, and she clenched her fist. It'd be cute if she was kidding, but she wasn't.

The other two looked at each other and rolled their eyes while Ming took a sip of water. "They had to shave off part of my hair to sew me up, so I started wearing wigs. It's grown back now, but I like having crazy hair." Her grin was infectious and helped Annie and Emir to relax. "My parents even let me get matching contact lenses that I wear when I want to make a statement. Pink hair and pink eyes are always a hit." They all laughed.

Emir turned toward Annie. He was intrigued by this girl who had fought off a shark, and he wanted to know more. There had to be a lot going on below the surface because she looked too plain and dumpy to be anybody's idea of a hero. "Why don't you tell us why we're really here?"

Chapter 4

Annie's hands started to shake. Would they believe her? She settled into her chair, shook her head slightly and began her story.

"When I died, I saw my father. He was in a Coast Guard unit that was in Afghanistan to improve relations with the local villagers. He was shot in the head six months ago as he was delivering supplies to a new girls' school that his team had just built." Her breathing was fast and shallow, and her lips started trembling, but she had to get it out. "He wasn't even a soldier. He was building a school!" She let out a low moan, bent over and buried her head in her hands.

Ming walked over, sat on the arm of the chair and hugged her. Emir couldn't hear what Ming was murmuring, but Annie eventually regained her composure. It took awhile because that was the first time that she had talked about her father's death with anyone other than her mother and her shrink.

Annie wiped her eyes, straightened her shoulders and got ready to continue. If Ming and Emir were going to ridicule her, there was nothing she could do about it. "Daddy told me to make his death mean something. I should change the world. Make it a better place. He said that I would find a way, and I think I have, but I need your help." She took a deep breath and gathered her thoughts.

"I absolutely believe that my experience was real. So, I started doing a lot of research. What I'm going to say might sound weird at first, but hear me out." She started grinning and talking with her hands. "It's so simple and marvelous that I can't even sleep at night. My brain just keeps coming up with all kinds of possibilities."

"Tell us!" Emir and Ming were sitting on the edge of their seats.

"You know how death changes a person—"

Emir and Ming gave a knowing chuckle.

"No, seriously, we all felt a connection with these other beings. An infinite number of connections."

The other two nodded in agreement.

Annie continued. "I think these connections exist among the living as well."

Ming interrupted her. "I'm Buddhist and that's part of our basic beliefs. How's that going to change the world?"

"I want to take it to a different level. The violence in the world is terrible. Every time you log in or hear the news, somebody's been murdered."

Ming sprang to her feet. "They're beheading people and filming it! Nobody's doing anything about it!"

Emir slammed his fist against his thigh. "Sometimes, I'm ashamed to be a Muslim. The terrorists are causing the rest of the world to hate all of us."

Ming waved her hands in front of his face. "What are you talking about? We don't hate you. We just met you, but you seem like a great guy."

Emir looked at the floor. "Religion should be a personal thing. Too many people are willing to kill in the name of whatever god they happen to believe in. Can't they see how stupid and barbaric that is?"

Annie chimed in. "Whatever they believe, at least three-quarters of the world believes something else."

Ming started pulling on her wig. "But it's not just terrorism and religious wars. Look at all the murders that happen in our cities every day. It's like a freakin' virus has infected people."

"Exactly! And I want to start a different kind of infection!" Annie clapped her hands in excitement, and her eyes began to gleam. Grinning broadly, she continued. "The adults are screwing up the world, so I'm going to start a kids' movement to fix it."

Ming and Emir both cried, "How?"

"We'll use social media to spread the word of peace. Encourage songwriters to write songs calling for a peaceful revolution. Fill people's consciousness with the idea of peace, and it'll spread like a virus."

"How do you know that?" Ming had trouble hiding her skepticism.

Annie was ready to defend her view. "Psychologists have done studies that show it works in cities. Enough local people think peaceful thoughts, and crime rates in their cities go down. I know it sounds far out. But, if we reach out to kids throughout the world to be part of the movement, I think we can make a difference."

Emir wasn't convinced, and a frown creased his handsome face. "How do we reach kids in countries without a lot of Internet? That's where most of the violence is now."

Annie threw her arms up in the air. "We use telepathy!"

"Oh, come on. That's nuts." Emir stood up and started walking around the room. "I agree that the social media campaign makes sense, but this is crazy."

Ming wanted to hear more. "Give her a chance to explain. Go ahead, Annie." Emir glared at her but remained silent.

Annie paused a minute to decide on the easiest way to talk about it. "I'll just give you the five-minute overview for now. Okay?"

They didn't object, so she continued. "Okay, what I'm going to say applies to the social media campaign as well as to how we can reach people in the isolated countries."

"You go, girl." Annie smiled at Ming's words of encouragement.

"Thoughts produce electrical brain waves. That's a scientific fact. It's also a fact that you can't destroy energy. So, if it can't be destroyed, where does all this brain-generated energy go?" Annie took a deep breath because this next part was the hardest to understand. "I think your brain acts like a radio station and broadcasts those electrical signals out into the air."

"Cool!" Ming just couldn't keep still and tried her best to ignore Emir's sneer.

"After reading tons of books and articles, I believe thoughts leave our body as energy that can be received by other people. Studies show that the most successful messages are sent as images by people who are physically close to the receiver."

Emir's face finally relaxed into a half grin. "Okay, I'm beginning to see where you're going with this."

Emir's words gave Annie the courage to continue. "So, if physical distance matters, we have to reach the kids in the Internet-connected countries that border the undeveloped regions."

Ming couldn't contain her enthusiasm. "This is the coolest thing ever! Count me in!"

Emir nodded. "I'm with you."

"So, we all agree? Somehow, we'll organize the kids around the world to send out visions of peace." Annie's relief filled the room.

Emir thought for a few moments. "There's a reason you beat that shark, Annie McDoogan." He started pacing and pulling on his ear. "Don't you have the magazine interview in a couple of days? Tell them what you've got in mind. It's a national audience."

Annie grinned. "What could go wrong?"

Chapter 5

Onward Christian soldiers... Annie woke with a start with that familiar tune running through her head. *What the heck?* She heard it again, surprised that it was real and not part of a dream. She buried her face in her pillow as she realized that the tune was their new doorbell ringer. This time her mother had gone too far. Sitting up, she heard familiar voices in the living room. *Oh, no.* Their parish priest had come to her interview. He must have been the one that installed the new doorbell.

Father John Sullivan had been part of Annie's life since the day he baptized her. When she was younger, she adored him and loved to listen to his Bible stories. As she grew older, he seemed more out of touch with the real world. The kids in her church wanted him to organize dances, tennis lessons and golf teams. Instead, he chose to spend his time teaching Bible study classes that few attended.

The more he appeared to bury his head in the sand, the more strident his sermons became. He didn't use to be this way, but the new pope was calling into question many of his established beliefs, and it left him feeling like he was drowning in quicksand. The harder he tried to hide his feelings of loss and abandonment, the more often they erupted in fiery outbursts.

Father John had always been a family friend and frequent dinner guest. But, since her father had died, he had started dropping by during the day and offering parenting advice to Colleen. Annie appreciated the fact that he was comforting her mother, but things were getting out of hand. In addition to new crucifixes appearing on the walls every week and the Bible assuming a place of honor on a pedestal in the living room, her mother had started wearing a rosary around her neck. Now their freakin' doorbell was encouraging Christians to engage in holy wars. Annie was fed up with the changes in her mother and their house.

The people from the magazine weren't due for another hour, so Annie took her time getting ready. She decided to wear her favorite Michio Kaku T-shirt with a pair of blue shorts. The photographer was going to do her makeup, so she didn't bother trying to hide her zits.

The doorbell rang again, setting Annie's nerves on edge. She'd take that stupid thing apart tomorrow, but right now, she had to focus on not making a fool of herself. Once the writer and photographer were inside, Annie made her appearance. After Maddie and Paul had introduced themselves, Paul had her sit at the dining room table while he fixed her hair and applied the makeup. She felt like a movie star as they walked back into the living room.

That feeling was brief. When Paul started taking close-ups of her wound, Annie's good mood evaporated as quickly as it had come. She was depressed and ready for a fight, and her mother was the perfect target.

Maddie started her tape recorder. "Okay, Annie, why don't—"

The time had come. "I'm not saying anything until my mom and Father John leave the room."

What now? There were times when Colleen didn't understand her daughter at all. "Annie—"

"No, Mom. Get out."

"Annie—"

"Get out! Either you leave or this interview is over!"

"But we have a contract."

"*You* have the contract, and *you* have the money. All *I* have is everybody seeing pictures of my ugly leg. Get out!" She stomped her good foot and started to leave.

Colleen shook her head in confusion, but she and Father John disappeared into the kitchen where they could still hear everything while remaining out of sight. She couldn't afford to have the contract canceled.

Maddie Greenwald was a short, plain woman dressed in drab clothes. Her dark hair was streaked with gray, and she wore no makeup. Maddie prided herself on her journalistic skills, but she felt like her talents were wasted interviewing teenagers for the magazine. Shark or no shark, she didn't see any potential here to hold her interest, and she was already planning a quick escape to catch some rays on the beach before her flight home. The fact that the kid appeared to be a spoiled brat added to her impatience. The photographer left to catch an early flight, and now it was just Maddie and Annie facing each other in the living room.

The first few minutes held no surprises as Annie talked about growing up in Fort Lauderdale, her father's death and the shark attack. The newspapers had covered this background information, so Maddie was already familiar with it. The next question, however, was the one Annie had been waiting for.

"You've been given a second chance at life. Has it changed you?"

Annie grinned. "You could say that. I saw my father when I was drowning, and he told me to change the world."

Maddie couldn't help but smile at Annie's exuberance. But, the smile was quickly replaced by a frown. "You lost me. Back up and slow down. You're telling me you had an out-of-body experience after the attack, and you saw your father?"

"Yes."

Maddie had heard many similar stories and had even interviewed a few of the survivors. However, reports of the deceased relatives talking to them were rare. "And he talked to you?"

"Not talking, exactly. More like flashing images. But, it was very clear what he wanted."

"And he told you to change the world?"

"I got the feeling that he wanted his death to mean something. So, the first thing I want to do is to organize kids around the world to unite and send out messages of peace."

"Why target kids?"

"Because their minds are more open to new ideas."

"Sending out messages of peace doesn't seem radical to me. People constantly pray for peace."

"And prayers don't seem to be working. You want Divine intervention, and I want direct intervention. We're going to do it telepathically." *Ta da!* Annie could almost hear her mother gasp.

Humph! This interview just got interesting. "What do you know about telepathy?"

"I know that people who have near-death experiences and some people who take psychedelic drugs feel a connection with other beings. In my case, I felt it with people who had died."

"Okay... "

"Think of the universe as a giant power grid that's laid out like a spider web. Everything on it is connected to everything else. Thoughts leave our body as packets of energy and travel along this web." Annie noticed Maddie's frown and became defensive. "Nothing in this idea violates the laws of physics."

"I'll take your word for it." Maddie glanced down at her notes for a minute before continuing. "So, you think there's an infinite number of thoughts moving around in the ether."

Annie clapped her hands. "Exactly! Some people call this the universal consciousness."

"And you think you can use this?"

"Yes! I want to tap into it. Studies show that when large numbers of individuals concentrate on sending out peaceful images, the crime rate in the surrounding areas drops."

"So, receiving images of peace makes people less violent?"

"It appears to. Perhaps the positive energy they're receiving affects the chemistry of their brains and calms them. If someone is surrounded by violence and anger, that negative energy may trigger their own anger. If we change the consciousness around them so that there's more peaceful energy than violent energy, we may be able to change their behavior."

Maddie nodded. "It sounds like you're going to need a lot of people working together if this has any chance of succeeding."

Annie threw both arms up in the air. "Yes! That's why we want to get the kids around the world to help us. We can't do it without them."

I'll be darned. She may be on to something, and it could be just the boost my career needs. "Maybe my magazine can help. We have offices around the world and publish in five different languages." Maddie paused a moment to write herself a note. "They may agree to reprint this article. Let me talk to my editor, and I'll get back to you. Meanwhile, you should set up a website so that volunteers can reach you. Let me know when you have a domain name, and I'll add it to the article."

Annie got up, limped over to Maddie and hugged her. "Thank you." Suddenly, they could hear angry voices coming from the kitchen.

Annie was hobbling over to see what was going on when Father John burst from the kitchen, his eyes wild with rage. He was shouting something about blasphemy and sacrilege. Colleen was yelling from the kitchen, and as he turned to face her, he accidentally pushed Annie. She lost her balance and hit the tile floor hard on her bad leg.

"Mommy!" She started to pant as the pain threatened to overwhelm her, and she fought off the priest's attempts to help her up as she screamed in agony.

Colleen rushed to her daughter's side and cradled Annie's head in her lap, cooing softly in her ear. Father John looked down at the tableau and for a moment, he was saddened by the fact that he would never have children. However, as Annie continued to scream, he was also relieved.

Colleen looked at her friend with sadness clouding her eyes. "John, you have to leave." Annie heard her mother's words and briefly sighed in relief before passing out.

Colleen had almost forgotten that Maddie was still there, but now it was time to end this interview. "My daughter's experienced things in the past six months that no 15-year-old should have to deal with. Her father was murdered, and a shark almost killed her. I believe it's all been too much for her and that she's suffering from delusions. You can print what you want, but I'm taking her to see her psychiatrist tomorrow. I think my baby is having a nervous breakdown. There's no other logical explanation for these crazy ideas."

Maddie gave a sympathetic nod but was glad her tape recorder was on. This was going to make a juicy story, and she was going to milk it for all it was worth.

Chapter 6

Dr. Lamberti enjoyed working with teens, and Annie was one of her favorite patients. Annie was bright, caring and possessed natural charisma. There was nothing pretentious about her, and she didn't care what other people thought about her. Most kids want to fit in, but not Annie. All Annie wanted was to win the Nobel Prize in Physics someday.

That thought made Dr. Lamberti smile. Annie reminded her of her younger self. Except she would never have had the guts to fight a shark. Annie was a remarkable girl.

Annie's world had fallen apart when her father died, but she had been on the road to recovery. Now, according to Colleen McDoogan, Annie had relapsed. It was time to bring her in and find out what was going on. She hit the buzzer that unlocked the door to the waiting room, leaned back in her padded chair and waited for her patient to enter.

"What's up, Doc?" They both grinned at Annie's usual greeting.

"I hear you've been busy. Fighting a shark and starting a revolution."

Annie rolled her eyes. "Been talking to my mom?"

Dr. Lamberti waited for Annie to continue. "It's not a revolution. It's a movement. I want to try to stop the violence in the world since the adults just keep messing it up."

"You think you can save the world?"

"Yes. Why not? One person has always been able to light a fire that changes society. I don't think what I want to do is impossible."

"What gave you the idea?"

"I saw my father when I drowned, and I saw him again last night."

Last night? This was news. "How did you see your father last night?"

"In a dream. I was thinking about quitting after Father Sullivan knocked me down and went ballistic. Daddy showed up and told me to stick to it."

"You heard him?"

"No, I just knew what he wanted."

"How are you sleeping these days?" Annie had borrowed some relaxation tapes after her father had died in order to get to sleep.

"Not good. My brain just won't get still. I have new ideas all the time, and I keep thinking about them all night."

Dr. Lamberti paused a moment to write some notes on her pad. "Try drinking some camomile tea before you go to bed. That might work, and I'll let you borrow the tapes again."

"Okay, but it's kind of cool to have ideas keep you awake."

"I want you to try and calm down. You realize that a lot of religious people may have the same reaction as your parish priest?"

Annie chewed the end of her pigtail for a few minutes while she considered the doctor's words. Her shoulders slumped as she stared at the carpet. "But this has nothing to do with religion. I don't understand why Father John was so upset."

"From what your mother told me, you plan to tell people that prayer is useless, and—"

"Probably not useless, but it's not enough. Turn on the TV. All you hear about is people being killed."

Dr. Lamberti waited a few seconds for Annie to calm down. "Okay, but can you understand why this might upset some people?"

Annie grimaced. "As long as they don't knock me down, I'll be okay."

The psychiatrist put down her pen, reached out and took Annie's hand. "These people can be violent. You may be in danger."

Annie hung her head. "I have to do what daddy wants me to do. He won't let me get hurt."

The doctor tightened her grip. "Annie, don't do this now. You need more time to heal, both physically and emotionally. Wait six months and see if you still want to do it."

She lifted her chin and looked straight at her doctor. "No."

The doctor pulled her hand back and sighed. "Do you plan to do this alone?"

Annie kicked the floor. "No, that would be crazy. There are three of us."

Dr. Lamberti struggled to keep from laughing. This is the reason she enjoyed working with kids. They knew no boundaries. If Annie believed three teenagers could bring peace to the world, all she could do was caution her. She obviously wasn't going to be able to change Annie's mind.

"Your story and photo will soon appear in a national magazine, so it's too late to protect your own privacy. If your two friends want to be on the frontline, that's their choice. Just don't put other people in danger. Particularly, the kids who join the movement."

Annie gave a slight grin. "Okay. But, that's not all of it."

"What else is there?"

Annie took a deep breath. "Once the peace movement is firmly established, I want to continue to explore how extrasensory perception and the connections between people can be applied to make the world a better place."

"What do you mean?"

Annie started picking at her face before she answered. "I think some normal people know how to channel the energy in their body to accomplish extraordinary things. Holy men in India and China have been developing this power for thousands of years, but they keep their techniques secret, and the western world somehow just discounts the whole thing. I want to focus on a portion of this. It's part of who we are. It's our birthright. Even the Dalai Lama is urging scientific research into psychic phenomena."

Dr. Lamberti stared at the ceiling as she digested Annie's words. "I understand that. Why do you think the holy men's methods haven't been made public?"

Annie sighed. "Because the power can be abused and used for evil purposes." She shrugged. "But that's how it is with anything good. There's always a flip side. That doesn't mean you keep it in the shadows."

Annie's voice grew louder as she became more insistent. "We have the right to explore its potential. Religious people might say that God wouldn't have given us this gift if He didn't want us to use it. Otherwise, what's the point?"

Dr. Lamberti sat and stared at her young patient. On her pad, she wrote:

hallucinations?
trouble sleeping?
delusions of grandeur?
schizophrenia?

Chapter 7

Annie, Ming and Emir stayed in touch through email and decided to meet at Annie's house to plan the next steps while Colleen was out showing property. Annie wanted to keep their meetings secret because things at home were tense enough already.

Emir was the first to arrive, and his dazzling smile made Annie's heart race. She hoped that he didn't notice her trembling hands when she invited him in. As they waited for Ming, they talked about the priest's reaction, but it didn't seem to worry him. When Ming finally got there, she was sporting a bright orange wig, hoop earrings and orange contact lenses. She looked like a cute alien.

Annie and Emir laughed as they took it all in. Ming was relieved that the meeting was going to start on a good note because she wasn't sure how they were going to react to her latest brainstorm.

"Hi guys, sorry I'm late. I was finishing up some research on the greatest idea ever." Ming wasn't afraid to praise herself. But, the other two didn't mind. It was part of her charm.

Emir looked skeptical. "We'll be the judge of that."

Ming laughed, glad that she had caught his attention. "No, really. It's amazing that nobody's thought of it before. Who knew? I'm a genius." She was hopping from one foot to the other in her excitement to tell them.

Emir spoke up again. "I bet your new-found intelligence will come as a surprise to your parents."

Annie grinned and intervened. "Okay, you two. Go ahead, Ming, before you sprain an ankle."

"I think we should push to have movie and television producers include a subliminal image of peace. Like they do with pictures of popcorn boxes as you're sitting in a theater waiting for a movie to start. The image flashes too quickly for your eyes to see it, but it registers in your brain and plants the idea in people that they want popcorn. How could anybody object to this?"

She twirled around on her tiptoes before continuing. "We already have a version of it. Now, it can be used to modify a different type of behavior. This is the virus we need. We plant the seed in everyone who watches movies and television, and that's pretty much the entire world. Maybe some of the producers would even display the image when they roll the credits. Genius." She threw her arms up in the air in pure delight.

Emir and Annie sat speechless on the couch as they watched Ming dance around the room. Finally, she sat down and looked at them, waiting for a reaction.

Annie spoke first. "But that's an entirely different approach than what we've been talking about. There are only three of us. How are we going to manage it?"

"I'll write the letters to the studio and network heads, directors and producers. Maybe some of them will want to meet me and end up casting me in a movie." Ming's eyes were sparkling.

Emir frowned. "So, that's why you want to do this."

Ming glared at him. "No, but it would be a nice fringe benefit. World peace plus a movie career. What's your problem?"

"I don't have a problem, but you've got the attention span of a gnat, and you're never going to follow through on this."

Ming jumped up and shook her fist at him. "You don't know me! I will too do it!"

"All right. Stop it. Ming, it's a great idea. Emir, quit baiting her. We've only got an hour before mom gets home, so how are we going to do this?"

Emir answered her. "I'll work with you to get the website up and running, and Ming can write her letters. When does the magazine article come out?"

Annie scratched her head. "In a couple of weeks, I think. I need to send Maddie a name for the movement and a domain name for the website, so she can include them in the article."

Emir stroked his chin. "How about Change Our World, and the domain name can be change-our-world dot com?"

"Perfect! Ming, you okay with it?"

Ming shrugged. "I don't care."

Annie knew her feelings were hurt. "Ming, do you have any idea what kind of image we can use?"

She perked up. "I forgot! That's the other thing I have to tell you. I think we should incorporate different cultural symbols of peace into one image. For example, a white dove symbolizes peace in Christianity, Islam and Judaism, and the V sign is recognized around the world, including Japan and China, as a symbol of peace. So, if we superimpose a white dove with a V, I think that should do it."

Emir was impressed and repentant. "Amazing. I wouldn't have thought of that. You're very creative. We make a good group."

Ming smiled. "You're forgiven. You can make it up to me by taking me to a movie."

Annie didn't like the way that conversation was going. "Okay, let's stay on track. So, we ask kids to focus on that image, and movie and TV producers to flash it. How do we keep everybody safe from the fanatics?" Dr. Lamberti's warnings were still fresh in Annie's mind.

Emir had already been thinking about the risk. "I'll design the website, so there are no chat rooms, and no way for the visitors to post. It will just be information about what we're trying to do. I'll upload Ming's peace image, but it will be up to them to organize themselves into groups with people they trust. The site will stress the risk and urge them to keep it secret. That's the best I can do."

Ming clapped her hands. "Maybe we can sell some things on the website and make a little money."

Annie nodded. "Okay, try to come up with some merchandising ideas." She stood up and walked toward the front door. "We know what we have to do. Let's hope everybody loves the magazine article."

Chapter 8

Splat... splat, splat! The unusual sounds woke Annie, and she opened her window to see if it was hailing. *Splat!* An egg broke against the window frame, showering her with runny yellow yolk.

"Blasphemer!"

"Satan!"

It didn't take long for Annie to figure out that the magazine must have hit the newsstands that morning. Interestingly, it was adults who were outside, and not kids, even though the article was published in a teen magazine. She flipped them the bird, shut the window, washed her face and went in search of her mother.

She found her in the kitchen talking on the phone with the Coral Springs police department. Colleen's voice was calm, which was a good sign, but Annie could tell by her posture that she was upset and frustrated. When the going got tough, they both turned into slouchers. Annie was surprised that they hadn't developed hunchbacks by now.

Colleen turned to face her daughter and sighed. "They're going to send a patrol car by to run the people off, and they'll keep an eye on the house for the next few days. Looks like the magazine article is attracting attention. I'll go out later and pick up a copy."

Annie was just starting to realize the full implications of her actions. "You should probably go to another city where you're not going to run into anybody you know." She took a bite of a chocolate donut. "I'm sorry, Mom. I didn't think they'd come to the house."

Colleen shook her head. "What's done is done. Just try to keep a low profile, okay?"

"Oh, let me check the website."

Colleen was startled. "You have a website? How did you do that?"

"Emir did it. Hey, look, we've had 1,000 hits already! They can't post anything, so I'll need to pull up the email." Annie was silent for a few minutes. "Oooh, we have about 300 emails. It looks like it's split 50/50 between good and bad. I'll have to answer some of the positive ones and let Emir and Ming know what's going on. We can take turns answering these."

Colleen chewed an antacid tablet as she watched her daughter hunched over the keyboard. She was so like her father, headstrong and willing to fight for her beliefs. It was one of the reasons she had married him, but it made her afraid for her daughter. Annie wanted to make a difference in the world. Was she delusional or could she actually pull it off? Colleen agreed with many of the protesters' sentiments. She was a religious woman and felt that Annie's telepathy approach discounted the value of prayer and God's influence. She prayed that He would watch over her daughter. But, she wouldn't leave it entirely in His hands. Colleen would do everything in her power to protect her. Delusional or not, Annie was all she had.

Annie let her mind wander as she and her mother sat in their regular pew during Sunday Mass. It had been an eventful week. The cops kept people away from the house, and Maddie Greenwald called and told her the article had lit up their phone lines. Most of the calls were complaints, but any publicity was good publicity, so the publisher decided to release it worldwide. Now, the kids needed to find volunteers to translate their web pages into different languages and answer the foreign emails. Her shadow army was growing, and she was smiling when the sound of her name caught her attention. Father Sullivan had started his sermon.

"Annie McDoogan recently gave an interview in which she stated that prayer was ineffective, so she was going to start a movement to control people's minds. As Catholics, you know that we all have free will. This is the work of the devil!" Father Sullivan's face was flushed as he warmed to his subject. "I know Annie is a good girl, and this isn't her fault. Something's taken hold of her soul and led her down the wrong path. Let's all bow our heads and say a prayer for Annie."

Annie squirmed in her seat, embarrassed beyond words as people turned and stared at her. This was something she didn't see coming, and the sight of all those lowered heads infuriated her. Church or no church, she wasn't going to take this abuse. Her mother threw her arm across her chest in a futile effort to hold her back, but Annie was having none of it.

She jumped to her feet and pointed her finger at the priest. "You have no right to say those things! I'm trying to bring peace to the world in the only way I know how!"

Father Sullivan recited his canned reply. "Pray to God, and He will lead you."

"Look at the world! Look at all the damage that's been done in the name of religion. Believe what you want to believe, but I will never think that encouraging people to think peaceful thoughts is evil! Maybe God will intervene and help those messages reach the right people. Or maybe He won't. It doesn't matter! What I'm doing has nothing to do with religion! If you're too blind to see that, then maybe you're the one who's possessed."

The congregation gasped. Nobody ever talked to Father Sullivan that way. At least not in public. A few kids clapped and were immediately silenced by their parents. Then, former classmates of Annie's stood up in a show of solidarity.

"Get out. Get out of here now and don't come back!" The priest was beyond angry.

The kids ignored him. One of the older boys started drumming on the back of the pew in front of him. Other kids joined in and soon the church was rocking. One girl in the choir began singing John Lennon's *Imagine* while another choir member picked up his guitar and started strumming out the tune.

Even the adults were caught up in the magic of the moment, and sounds of peace filled the church. The revolution had begun.

Chapter 9

Someone reported the incident at the church to the local news channel, and Annie, Emir and Ming were booked to appear on Thursday night's local issues show. The hate mail was escalating, and Annie was apprehensive about bringing the other two into the spotlight, but they insisted. In a way, she was relieved. She hated public speaking and having Ming and Emir there would take the pressure off her to be entertaining. Ming volunteered to do Annie's makeup and agreed to keep it conservative. Later in the week, the two of them were going to meet at the mall to try and find Annie an outfit for the show that didn't make her look frumpy. Colleen was happy to give her some of the magazine money for shopping. She was glad that Annie finally had a friend even though she didn't agree with their goals.

Father Sullivan's verbal attack on Annie inspired a lot of kids from her parish to form a well-organized group in support of her. One of their favorite activities was bombarding the priest with mental images of

Ming's peace symbol to see if they could change his attitude. Annie suspected that some of the older kids were also sending sexy images just to mess with his head.

Thursday finally arrived, and Ming came over at noon to help Annie get ready for the show. It took her two hours, but the results were worth it. She looked cute and felt like a million bucks. They hugged when Ming left and agreed to meet Emir at the television studio at six o'clock.

The hours flew by, and Annie was a nervous wreck by the time she arrived at the studio. She was relieved to see that Ming wasn't wearing tinted contact lenses that matched her purple hair. They were surprised at how many teens were in the audience until the show's director explained that some of the schools offered extra credit to students who attended this weekly local news show.

Emir was late, which was unusual for him, and when he finally arrived, he appeared sullen and withdrawn. Annie wanted to ask him what was wrong, but the show was ready to start, and the director asked them to take a seat on the couch next to the host's desk.

Ming made a beeline for the spot next to the desk, but Emir gracefully blocked her path and pushed Annie into the prime seat next to the host. Emir sat next to her, and Ming was left with the end seat. She was happy to be sitting next to Emir, but not pleased to be so far away from the microphone.

The first few minutes focused on a discussion of how they came together, and all three got a chance to tell their story. After the commercial, the conversation veered toward the website, and Emir found him-self answering most of the questions. Then, Annie was asked about Father Sullivan's behavior, and that topic chewed up a significant chunk of time. Ming was fidg-eting and feeling like a second fiddle. After the next commercial, she decided to shake things up. Leaning forward in her seat, Ming had a clear view of the host. Before the moderator could start a new discussion, Ming jumped in.

"Excuse me, but there's a subject we haven't talked about yet."

"Oh?"

"Yes. While Emir and Annie are reaching out to kids, I'm contacting television producers, movie direc-tors, and heads of studios and networks."

The moderator sat up straighter in her chair. "Why would you contact them?"

Ming smiled. "We thought that they could include subliminal messages and images of peace in mov-ies and TV shows. That way, the idea gets directly in viewers' brains, and one movie can reach millions of people. They do it now to get people in the theater to buy refreshments. This seems like a more worthwhile cause and is easy to do."

"Isn't this something they would prefer to do in se-cret?"

Ming pushed out her lower lip and hung her head. "Nobody answered my letters, so I have no choice but to take it public."

"Don't you think people will object to this type of mind control?"

"Everybody knows they already do it with snacks, and it doesn't stop people from going to the movies. Who's going to say they don't want peace? The entire civilized world wants peace."

"That's true, but people have rights."

Ming had done her homework and anticipated this question. "There are no laws regarding mental rights."

"Hmm. Good point. You're welcome to come back anytime and keep us updated on your progress. It sounds like an idea worth pursuing." The host rubbed her forehead as she considered how to top this revelation. They still had ten minutes left in the show. "Anything else you want to share?"

Did she dare? Heck, yes. This chance may never come again. She looked at Emir and Annie, and they appeared to be holding their breaths. Their expressions made her hesitate for a moment, but the entertainer inside her couldn't resist this once-in-a-lifetime opportunity. "Well, I've written a peace song." She turned in her seat to talk to the audience. "Anybody want to hear it?"

The audience responded enthusiastically. "Sing it, girl!"

The moderator checked the time. "We'll be right back after this commercial break with Ming Chang singing her original song."

The audience clapped as they broke for the commercial. Ming asked for a guitar, and they located one in the back room. The microphone stand was set up in center stage, and Ming was ready to go when the camera's red light started to blink. She looked straight ahead and didn't glance at Emir and Annie. But, she could feel their unhappiness. They had no idea she had written a song.

"Ladies and gentlemen, here is Miss Ming Chang, singing her new song *Save Our World.*"

The clapping and wolf calls made her feel happier than she had ever felt in her life. She strummed a few chords, took a deep breath and prepared herself to wow them.

Help us shape our destiny
So we can save humanity
The choice is ours to win or lose

How many innocents must die
Before the world unites and cries
We need to live less painfully

Help us shape our destiny
So we can save humanity
Think peaceful thoughts and peace will come

Let's stand as one against our foe
Our lives are ours to shape and mold
To live in peace we must be bold

Help us shape our destiny
So we can save humanity
This violence is insanity

The Universe can overcome
The evil thoughts can be undone
To save the world we must unite

Help us shape our destiny
So we can save humanity
The silent fight will prove our might

Let anger cease and kindness thrive
We still have time to turn the tide
The Universe is on our side

Think peaceful thoughts and peace will come
The evilness can be undone!

The audience was cheering, "Do it again!" So Ming started singing it one more time as the show ran the closing credits. She was joyous and compelling. Emir and Annie were stunned.

Suddenly, there was a commotion in the seats! A man stood up. Raised his arm. People started yelling. A shot rang out... and the song died.

Chapter 10

Annie leaped off the couch and started running toward the fallen Ming. But, Emir was faster. His adrenaline was surging as he swung Annie up into his arms and carried her off stage.

She struggled to break free as he gently put her down while he kept hold of her arm. "What are you doing? I've got to help Ming!"

He whispered in her ear. "Be quiet! We don't know if they caught the shooter or if there's anybody else out there." Annie looked up at his worried face as he planned his next move. "We may be targets too. Go hide in the back room, and I'll go get Ming."

She knew he had to do it because there was nobody else who would. She rubbed his arm. "Be careful."

He stroked her hair and took off, running in the jagged fashion he had seen men do in movies when they were trying to avoid getting shot. He could hear the faint sound of sirens over the screams of kids. Ming was alone on center stage, and a quick glance was enough to convince him that the bullet had hit her arm, and it was safe to pick her up. She had a glazed look in her eye and was unresponsive. He tore his sleeve off and wrapped it around her wound.

"Ming, you've been shot, and I'm going to pick you up and carry you off stage. Can you hear me?"

She was silent but looked at him with fear in her eyes.

"Okay, put your good arm around my neck and hang on tight."

She gave a slight smile and did as he requested.

It was over in less than a minute. He effortlessly lifted her and ran as quickly as he could, crouching and weaving, back to Annie. He was out of breath as he whispered to Annie while he set Ming down on the top of a desk. "The cops are on the way. I could hear the sirens. She was shot in the arm, but it doesn't look too bad. Text everybody and let them know we're all right."

Emir quickly scanned the room. "Come on, get under this table and be quiet. We don't know where the shooter is." He carried Ming and gently set her down in front of the table. "Go ahead, crawl in. Annie, get over here and get in there with her. I'm going to look for a cover."

He found an old blanket that he threw over the table and crawled in with the girls. Ming was whimpering that her arm hurt. "Shhh. Be quiet. The cops will be here in a minute."

Thump, thump, thump. They froze at the sound of footsteps coming toward them. *Thump, thump, thump. Click.* The lights were on! *Clack, clack, clack.* Someone in high heels running. Their pounding hearts sounded like cannons. The girls grabbed each other's hand. Sweat was pouring off their bodies. Emir was getting ready to lash out at the attacker.

"Annie?"

They started trembling with relief, and Annie lifted the blanket. "Mommy?"

"It's over. Come on out."

The trio crawled out to see Colleen and a cameraman standing in the lit room. "Some of the high school football players tackled the gunman and are sitting on him until the cops get here. The security guard is trying to get them off, but they refuse to budge. It doesn't look as if there's anybody else involved. Just one man. A doctor in the crowd said he sounded like a schizophrenic who was off his meds." Colleen paused for a minute to look at Ming's arm. "They kept the cameras rolling the whole time. It went out live."

Colleen chatted with them for a while until the paramedics arrived to take Ming to the hospital. Emir received permission to ride along with her to keep her calm until her parents made it to the emergency room. Ming smiled as he sat down beside her. Even though she was in pain, she couldn't pass up such a perfect opportunity to flirt.

She reached out with her good arm and took his hand. "Thank you for what you did. You're the bravest person I've ever known."

He gave her hand a slight squeeze and put it back in her lap. "Anybody would have done the same."

She shook her head. "Not true. Nobody was rushing up on stage to protect me. Just you."

Emir laughed. "And Annie. She ran right for you. I had to carry her off. I can't afford to get you both shot." He laughed again. "Nobody would be around to annoy me."

She stroked his hand and spoke in a soft, seductive voice. "I don't want to annoy you."

Once again, he returned her hand to her lap and smiled. "Behave! You're supposed to be anxious and in shock."

Ming smiled and batted her eyelashes. "Oh, I'm anxious all right."

Emir looked through the back window and saw Ming's parents standing at the emergency entrance. "Hey, we're here." He jumped out as soon the doors opened. "Text us when you're released. I'm going over to Annie's." Ming blew him a kiss and chose to ignore the sound of relief in his voice.

Colleen ordered a pizza and talked with them in the kitchen for a few minutes. Once she assured herself that they were recovered enough to eat, she went into the living room to watch TV.

Annie let out a sigh. "This isn't what I want. It's getting too big. Too dangerous. I think it's getting out of hand." She started chewing on her hair. "We were shot at!" She stood up and paced around the room. "I can't manage this."

Emir looked at her in the dimmed recessed lighting. "Then I'll manage it. Ming has some good suggestions, Annie. Flashing peace words and images in movies and television shows is pure brilliance, and I think her idea about selling things from the website is a good one too. We spend hours answering emails. We should get paid something for our time."

Annie snickered. "When did you start worrying about money?"

Emir was silent for a few moments. "My parents threatened to cut off my allowance if I showed up tonight. That's why I was late. But, here I am."

"Why didn't they want you to do it?"

"They're embarrassed about the movement and don't want their patients knowing I'm involved."

Annie smiled. "Well, now you're a hero, and all their patients know it. No worries. You're back in the gravy."

He ran his fingers through his hair. "That's the problem. I feel like they're trying to buy my loyalty." He strummed his fingers on the table. "To use it to manipulate me into doing what they want."

Annie patted his arm. "I think most parents try to control their kids any way they can. In your case, it's money. In mine, it's guilt." She shrugged.

"But it goes deeper than that. They have my whole life planned out. It drives me crazy!"

Annie looked at this beautiful, suffering boy beside her. "If you don't like it, change it. Save your money. Get an athletic scholarship. You're good at everything you do. You'd probably qualify in tennis, swimming or golf. Choose one and make your own way."

He smiled at her. "Thanks." He reached for a slice of pizza. "You're really good for me."

Annie blushed and changed the subject back to the events of the night. They talked and ate for an hour until Emir stood up and got ready to leave.

Emir sighed. "I wish we knew what was going to happen."

Annie's face broke out in a broad grin. "I know people who can tell us. It's time for a road trip!"

Chapter 11

School was out for the summer, and Emir picked the girls up at 7:00 Friday morning for the four-hour drive to Cassadaga. This Spiritualist town, which was established in 1894 as a safe haven for psychics, is located in Florida between Orlando and Daytona Beach. Annie had read remarkable stories of visitors' encounters, and she hoped that someone there could shed some light on their future success and safety. They had searched the mediums' biographies online and made appointments with three that were available Friday at noon. Emir and Ming were skeptical but thought it would be an interesting experience that they could all share in together.

Annie suggested that Ming sit up front since her arm was in a sling, and the front seat was more comfortable than the back. It would also make it easier for her to talk to Emir about what to sell on the website, which was a topic that held little interest for Annie. Besides, she hadn't been sleeping well and wanted to try and take a nap. She wasn't crazy about the idea of Ming sitting next to Emir, but he had chosen Annie as the first one to save, and that thought brought a slight smile to her lips. After one last look at the back of Emir's fine head, she drifted off to sleep.

The slowing of the car woke Annie, and she was surprised to see that they were already parked by the hotel. The town wasn't what she expected. Everything seemed so old and faded. It was clear that the residents had no interest in living a luxurious life.

They bought some chips and sodas at the hotel's restaurant and wandered around town for an hour, talking about the recent events. Annie wanted to stop all public appearances. She thought it was just too dangerous to continue. However, Ming and Emir overruled her, and she reluctantly agreed to continue.

Ming's song and shooting had been uploaded to the Internet and quickly went viral. Musicians were talking to her about covering the song. They would pay her royalties from the sales and had the right to change the music and tweak the lyrics. Her name would be on the label as the songwriter, which meant almost as much to her as the money. In addition, Maddie Greenwald had been in touch with her and was going to fly down in a couple of weeks to interview Victim Ming and Hero Emir. Shark Girl was old news. The girls who read her teen magazine would swoon over Emir.

Meanwhile, one of the national morning talk shows wanted to fly all three of them to New York next week to tape an appearance. Ming was thrilled and was already planning on catching a Broadway matinee while they were there. It was fun trying to decide on a show that they all wanted to see. Emir wanted a drama, and Ming was begging them to pick a musical. Annie suspected Emir was pushing for the drama just to rile Ming up and that he would eventually give in and agree to her wishes. It would be a fun trip, and their parents were going to let them go unchaperoned because the network was providing them with a limousine and driver for the day. Annie was hoping the network would also agree to pay for the matinee tickets and a fancy meal.

The hour passed quickly as they toured the town, and it was soon time for their appointments. They agreed to meet back at the restaurant when the sessions were over.

Annie rocked slowly back and forth on the weather-beaten porch as she waited for her session to start. She winced as the sound of a crying woman escaped from inside the medium's house. In a few minutes, a young woman came out, dabbing her swollen eyes. She didn't look at Annie and kept her head down as she stepped into the dusty street. The woman behind her introduced herself as Marilyn Jackson, and she invited Annie to come in and sit at her kitchen table that was next to the door. The walls prevented Annie from seeing into any of the other rooms.

Marilyn was a short, attractive woman with shoulder-length dark hair. She had a calm, loving expression on her face as she took both of Annie's hands. She held them palms up for a few moments and looked surprised when she released them.

"You're an unusual girl."

Annie nodded. "I suppose so."

"You've crossed over and returned." It was a statement and not a question.

Annie nodded again. "I drowned and was resuscitated."

"Ah... I see." Her next words shocked Annie. "You saw your father."

Annie jerked upright in her chair. "How do you know that?"

Marilyn smiled. "Your father is here. He loves you very much, but he says you have to try harder. Does that make sense to you?"

Annie put her head down on her folded arms and cried. Marilyn continued to talk, but nothing registered with Annie. She was overwhelmed by grief. After a few minutes, she lifted her head. "Did he suffer?"

"No, he died instantly. He was holding a schoolbook and thinking of you."

Annie's eyes started to water. "Is he going to keep me safe?"

Marilyn shook her head. "You're in great danger. I see a gray truck."

That puzzled Annie. She didn't know anybody that owned a truck. "Will I succeed?"

Marilyn frowned. "It's not clear, but your father is pointing to a white robe and a large ring."

Ming was a few minutes late for her reading because she stopped at the bookstore and lost track of time. When her medium opened the door, she looked upset although she quickly recovered her composure after touching Ming's good shoulder.

"My name's Karen Philippi. Come in." The door opened into an entrance hall, which contained a card table and two padded chairs.

Karen was an older woman with gray hair and faded blue eyes. Ming picked her after reading her online bio that said she was a singer and songwriter. Karen smiled. "You have a strong positive energy." She paused and seemed to be intent on something in the room. "A young man wants you to know that he forgives you."

Ming was surprised. "Forgives me for what?"

Karen was no longer smiling. "The accident."

Ming's jaw dropped, and she was speechless for the first time in her life. "How do you know that?"

"He's here in the room with us."

No. No. No. No. No. "That's impossible!"

Karen shook her head. "He wants to reach out to you and let you know that he's safe and in a good place."

Ming was in shock and searched for something to say. She didn't want to talk about the accident. "Am I safe?"

Karen paused for a moment. "I see water."

"Anything else?"

"No, just water. Be careful around water."

Ming needed to hear something more concrete. "Can you tell me about my career? Will I be famous?"

Karen smiled. "I think you already are. I saw you on the news. Good song."

Ming was delighted. "Thank you. That means a lot coming from you. But, will I be rich?"

Karen reached over and gently patted Ming's hand. "After much sorrow, you'll be happy."

Emir chose George Monroe because he had lived in Cassadaga for the past 30 years. He figured if the guy could make a living doing psychic readings for that long, he must be the real deal. They were meeting in one of Harmony Hall's back rooms. The medium didn't show any sign of recognition as he held onto Emir for a long handshake before inviting him to sit at the table.

George stared at Emir. "There's a cloudiness in your aura. You're a survivor, but the scars go deep. You need to correct this, or your energy will stay blocked. You will never be the man you're capable of being until this is fixed."

Emir exhaled deeply. "Yes, there are scars."

"You tried to hurt yourself."

Emir was becoming impatient. He didn't want to talk about his past. "What will I become?"

"A healer."

"Will that make my parents happy?"

"No."

Emir's face fell. "So, I can't win." He scratched his chin. "Will I be safe?"

George shook his head. "Someone you love is in danger. I see a man with a purple scarf."

Emir became agitated. "Something's going to happen to my parents?"

George held his arms open wide. "All I can see is a man and a purple scarf. I don't know the source. Be on guard."

Annie was the first to arrive after her session and chose a table in a deserted corner of the restaurant. She was glad to have a few minutes alone to unwind and recover from the shock of what she had just been through.

She was lost in her thoughts when Emir and Ming, looking disturbed and slightly glassy-eyed, joined her. They sat in silence until the waitress brought over glasses of water and asked for their orders. At that point, they realized how hungry they were and quickly scanned the menus.

Once they were alone again, Ming was the first to speak. "OMG, that was freakin' amazing. I wish I'd recorded it because I'll never remember all of it. She did recognize me from the news clips, and that may have given her an extra advantage even though we made the appointments using fake names and—"

Emir interrupted her. "People were whispering as we walked around town, so some of them must have recognized us. My guy didn't seem to know me, but he also told me things I had never mentioned to anybody."

Annie looked at Emir. "My lady didn't know who I was. I guess I blend in with the furniture. I'm not quirky like Ming or gorgeous like you. I'm just me."

Ming hugged her. "You're just a late bloomer. Once you stop wearing pigtails and get rid of the braces, everybody will notice you. Just don't get any more freckles."

Emir laughed. "Get as many freckles as you want. I like you fine just the way you are."

His kind words warmed her heart, and she was ready to talk about her session. "My father was in the room with us."

Emir gasped. "You saw him?"

"No, but he communicated with the psychic. It seemed to be by images. The same way I understood him in my near-death experience." She paused a moment to fully recall the painful experience. "He's disappointed in me."

Emir hit the table. "No!"

Ming was equally upset. "How can he say that?"

Annie wiped her eyes. "I'm not doing enough. I have to be stronger. The world is in danger, and I have to reach out to everybody." She sighed and put her head in her hands. "I can't do anything right."

Ming was outraged and sarcastic. "Maybe daddy will be happier when the international issues of the magazine are published. Will that get him off your back?"

Annie choked back a sob. "I don't know what he wants. Marilyn warned me about a gray truck, but I don't know what that means." Annie groaned and took a bite of her roast beef sandwich. "Enough about me. Either one of you get any warnings about danger?"

Emir tugged on his earlobe. "I wasn't going to mention it, but my psychic told me that someone was in danger from a man with a purple scarf."

Annie frowned. "A purple scarf? Who's in danger?"

"My parents, I think."

Annie looked at Ming. "Did you get any warnings?"

Ming was frowning. "She said I needed to be careful around water, but we mostly talked about music and what direction my career should take."

Annie pushed her chair back. "Well, if anything does happen, we can't say we weren't warned. Let's go home."

Chapter 12

The days flew by as Annie and Ming planned what to wear to New York for the national morning show. Ming was thrilled to be finally going to Manhattan, and Annie was thrilled to get another professional makeup job. It never ceased to amaze her how that girly side of her had appeared. Both girls interested Emir, so he was happy to come along.

The Manhattan news set was a gleaming mass of glass and chrome. There was no studio audience, but the entire back wall was a soundproof and bulletproof glass window looking out on Times Square. Outside monitors broadcasted the show to passers-by.

Emir had posted information about the upcoming interview on their website, so it wasn't entirely unexpected to see some kids gathered around the window. But, they were surprised to see that there were already about 50 teenagers standing outside in the summer heat, and it was still 40 minutes until showtime.

An assistant escorted the three teens to the makeup room, and the girls settled in to enjoy the pampering.

Emir refused to have his face powdered, so he sat in a chair behind them. Ming gave him a new white sling and a set of drawing pens and ordered him to draw peace symbols on the sling. He grunted but did as she asked, smiling slightly.

When they were called on set, they were amazed at the number of people in front of the window. There were hundreds! Some held "We love you Emir" posters while a fewer number rooted for Annie and Ming. Disturbingly, there were some negative signs as well. "Blasphemers" was a common one, and a few read "Go Back to Florida." Annie thought she saw Father Sullivan in the crowd, but she dismissed that as her imagination.

They sat around an oval glass table, so no one had to jockey for position. All three of the kids had an equal chance of being heard. Annie's seat, however, faced the window, and she found herself preoccupied with thoughts of the growing crowd outside.

Emir was the first to speak and explained the push to encourage kids to think about images of peace that hopefully would be received and calm the brains of individuals who might otherwise turn to violence. He then updated everyone on the success of the movement. Annie's magazine article had been published internationally the day before, and the website was now getting over 1,000 hits a day.

The crowd outside was getting rowdy. Girls (and a few boys) were kissing the window as Emir was speaking, and Annie noticed more negative signs pushing toward the front. Maybe she could calm them down.

Annie raised her index finger and waited for an acknowledgment from the host before she began to speak. "We need to come together for peace. Reacting with violence only creates more violence. Generals around the world are saying they want to bomb the terrorists to dust. They may succeed in killing many, but the violence will be used as a propaganda tool. For every person that's killed, more will step in as replacements."

The crowd seemed to quiet down, so Annie continued. "Poor young men are the target for recruiters, and these are the people we most need to reach with our images of peace. We must change the way they think. We must offer an alternative to violence."

Some in the crowd started cheering. "First, we have to reach them. We have to show them that there's no glory in brutality. We literally want to show them whether they like it or not. We have to send them images of peace." The crowd continued to push forward. "We must change the way they think or all is lost!" The crowd started chanting her name as she held up her hands for silence and relaxed in her chair.

Ming had been quiet for too long and started to speak as soon as Annie stopped. Her back was to the window, so she had to watch the monitors to gauge the crowd's reactions. "We need money to continue to reach out to people. We'll be posting information on the website next week. We also need multilingual volunteers to help us answer email. We can't do this without you." The crowd roared its approval, and some kids starting throwing dollar bills at the window.

Ming stared in amazement as a breeze caught the bills and lifted them up. Suddenly, there were hundreds of kids jumping in the air trying to catch the elusive dollars as they fluttered by. That was the last funny image she'd see for a while.

"Now, I want to speak to all the television and movie producers, studio heads, directors and film editors. We also need your help." The crowd settled down to listen. "You have in your hands the ability to reach millions of people around the globe. We are asking you to embed subliminal messages of peace in your movies and shows. It costs you nothing and has no affect on the quality of the film, but it will reach the hearts and minds of people everywhere." The crowd clapped. "You can coordinate this among yourselves. Reach out to your partners around the world. You can help make the world a better place. We need you!"

At that point, the chanting started. "Sing your song. Sing your song."

Ming glanced at the moderator who nodded and handed her a microphone so that she could stand in front of the window. She had a momentary flashback of the shooting but pushed it from her mind. She started slowly but gained confidence as she watched the crowd start to sing along with her. But, she also saw some teenagers jeering and trying to drown everyone else out.

Ming sang the song through once, and they begged for more. The moderator signaled that they were running out of time, so Ming just repeated the last two stanzas.

Let anger cease and kindness thrive
We still have time to turn the tide
The Universe is on our side

Think peaceful thoughts and peace will come
The evilness can be undone!

At the end, she was screaming the lyrics and raised her good arm high in the air. That's when the fighting broke out.

Fists were flying, and people were trampled. Even the girls were attacking each other. The commotion lasted a little over eight minutes until the Times Square police officers broke it up. A few of the instigators who were shouting "Pray to God" and "Only God can bring peace" were handcuffed and taken away. This time Annie was sure she saw her parish priest in the back of a police car defiantly staring at the camera crews that had quickly appeared on the scene. Perhaps a little too quickly.

Chapter 13

The limousine met Annie, Ming and Emir at the back entrance of the studio, so they avoided the possibility of being injured by the mob. Their spirits were momentarily dampened, but they quickly recovered. The driver stopped in midtown and let them out for a minute to buy Yankees baseball caps to help hide their faces. The caps, combined with their sunglasses, did a satisfactory job of disguising their identity. After Ming was shot, Annie had insisted that, except for public appearances, none of them disclose where they planned to be on any given day. Consequently, none of their fans (or enemies) knew the day's agenda.

They enjoyed a delicious lunch, courtesy of the network. However, the competition between Annie and Ming for Emir's attention was getting out of hand. Besides making idiots out of themselves in the limo, their seat-shuffling antics in the theater was a show in itself.

Annie pushed Emir in the row first, followed by her and then Ming. After a few minutes, Emir got up and went to the men's room. When he returned, Ming pressured Annie into scooting over so Emir would be sitting on the end next to her. Annie didn't like this turn of events, so she got up and went to the ladies room. When she returned, she had everybody slide over a seat. So, once again Emir found himself sitting between the two girls. He laughed to himself but didn't object.

They liked the musical and had almost forgotten the morning's chaos. Unfortunately, they arrived at the airport as the nightly news shows were starting their broadcasts. Television monitors were prominently positioned throughout the terminal, and as they checked in, they were treated with the vision of Ming singing her heart out to the crowd that morning. This was followed by video of the riot and police.

The kids pulled their caps down further over their eyes and hurried to their gate's waiting area. They sat side-by-side, facing the windows with their backs to the rest of the room.

They set their phones to receive the conservative news feed and prepared themselves to be simultaneously horrified and amused at the brainless comments. The word had apparently come down from the owner of the network to crucify them, and every newsperson used the exact same damaging phrases and buzzwords. The kids shook their heads in amazement that anyone could believe such asinine commentators. But, they knew they were in trouble as they listened to the remarks.

The first speaker they saw was a youngish blonde woman with big hair, plunging neckline and a push-up bra. Annie and Ming both snickered as they focused on what she was saying.

"A riot erupted this morning outside the ABC studio in Times Square. Police swarmed the plaza as an interview during the Morning Show incited the crowd to violence."

Annie hissed at her cell phone. "That's not fair!"

"Shh!" Ming and Emir didn't want to miss a word.

"Three teenagers from South Florida are developing a cult following among misguided teens who believe their message of using mind control to bring about peace in the world."

Ming, Emir and Annie all squirmed as they listened.

The commentator laughed. "They should have used some mind control on the crowd this morning."

Ming punched Emir's arm in frustration while Annie started chewing on her hair.

"The group is now asking for money, so they can spread their message. Do you really believe that? I think it's more likely they want the money to spend on entertaining themselves. Don't give these kids a dime!"

Emir groaned. "This isn't good, but it could be worse."

Clips of the fighting filled the screen as the commentator continued. "Now, to shed some more light on this issue is Annie McDoogan's parish priest, Father John Sullivan. Father?"

Annie gasped and texted her mother to watch. "Oh, crap! Here we go."

Ming cried out. "That man was outside my house last week. Just standing there staring. It was creepy."

Annie leaned over to look at Ming. "We stopped going to his church even though I think my mom secretly agrees with him. You should have your folks file a restraining order against him."

"Shh! He's starting to speak." Ming turned up the sound on her phone.

"I'm here today to warn the public of the evil that's among us. I baptized Annie and have watched her grow into a fine young lady. I'm here to tell you that this is not Annie McDoogan!" He shook his index finger for emphasis. "The devil entered her soul when she was most vulnerable. This child of God was nearly dead after a shark attack. She had no free will and no ability to make choices. Satan crept in and took over her body!"

Annie sighed. "I feel like I should stand up and shout Hallelujah!"

Father Sullivan was just getting warmed up. "I came here from Florida to save this girl's soul. To save her from the clutches of this demon."

Ming snorted. "Hey, what about the rest of us?"

The priest had no intention of ignoring the rest of the group. "The other two ring leaders of this so-called peace movement have a similar story. They both had serious accidents and lost control of their bodies. The dark forces entered them as well and now conspire to turn other innocent teenagers away from God and His eternal goodness."

Emir scratched his chin. "Why can't he understand what we're trying to do? I don't get it."

"These children are possessed by an evil power that tells them to use magic instead of prayer. They say that prayers are no good. Well, my brothers and sisters, we know better!"

Emir, Ming and Annie spoke as one. "It's not magic."

Father Sullivan leaned forward and looked directly into the camera. "We need to stop them any way we can."

With that remark, the interview ended. The kids ignored their ringing cell phones as they digested what they had just heard.

Emir was the first to speak. "You know, it sounded like he just ordered a hit on us."

Annie was visibly upset. "He didn't mean that. He just got caught up with all the attention and cameras."

That excuse didn't make Ming feel any better. "It doesn't matter if that's what he meant or not. This is a national show, and some nuts out there may take him seriously."

Emir had the last word as they were boarding the plane. "Our interview with Maddie is coming up, so we'll have a chance to get even. If he wants to play rough, we'll play rough."

Chapter 14

As Annie, Ming and Emir flew home, the Internet erupted in a storm of protest over Father Sullivan's remarks. Kids around the world united in their outrage against the man. A crowd gathered as word spread that two Fort Lauderdale teens were spray-painting the front of Father Sullivan's church. In almost no time, more than 200 kids stood laughing and partying alongside the caricature of the priest in a red jumpsuit with a Roman collar, horns on his head, a forked tail and a pitchfork facing an angelic sword-carrying Annie. The street swarmed with neighbors taking photos of the wall, and the pictures quickly went viral. Two of Annie's former classmates immediately got busy printing the image on T-shirts.

As the police car's blue light came closer, the kids formed a line, held hands and started chanting, "Father Sullivan wants to hurt us. Father Sullivan must go." Two officers tried to break it up but called for reinforcements as adults joined the line. By the time additional police arrived, the crowd had doubled in size, and bottles of alcohol were being passed around. The cops stayed in their patrol cars until bottles started being thrown against the church windows. At that point, a solid wall of blue approached the crowd urging everybody to break it up before anybody was hurt. The cautions only served to encourage the crowd to chant louder. Some of the girls started screaming, "We love you, Emir!"

A few minutes later, two mounted police arrived on the scene, and any more trouble was averted as the horses gently nudged their way through the crowd. Once the kids started petting them, the majority of the protesters went home.

The incident was the lead story on the local evening news, and viewers had a long look at the painting on the wall. The reporters did a good job explaining the peace movement and mentioning the priest's remarks earlier in the day. The group gained strong supporters that night.

Meanwhile, two of the national networks were feverishly preparing to capitalize on the day's events. No one could reach the kids or Father Sullivan, so alternatives had to be substituted. The conservative news station focused on lining up a televangelist for their evening talk show. It wasn't difficult finding someone who could arrive in New York in his private jet. The liberal news station, on the other hand, found a local Jesuit-priest who was willing to give his opinion of Father Sullivan's actions. The conservative show aired first.

"Fort Lauderdale, Florida, has become the unlikely center of a fight between good and evil. This normally quiet resort town erupted in violence this evening as the police arrested two teens for defaming a Catholic church. Here to comment is Tyler Marshall, a well-known Texas preacher and a frequent commentator on this network."

Pastor Marshall straightened his tie, took a sip of water and began to speak. "Thank you. I'm here this evening to lend my support to the Catholic priest who is fighting to save the soul of a young cult leader in South Florida. Some people have tried to demonize this man for his impassioned words, but I'm here to tell you that we should praise him! This poor girl has been taken over by the dark forces who are now trying to lead innocents away from praying to the Almighty God! My friends, this is a terrible thing that must be stopped!"

The preacher's voice rose in a crescendo. "Can you say, 'Help her, Jesus.'" He paused for a moment. "I can't hear you! Say it louder. 'Help her, Jesus, and deliver her soul from evil.' True believers must work together and silence her pagan words. God-fearing people can't allow this cult to grow any stronger. It's our duty to stop it. Amen, brothers and sisters, we'll fight this sacrilege together."

Jesuit priests don't own their own jets but are renowned for their intelligence and measured responses. Father Kevin McCarthy was no exception. He held doctorate degrees in psychology, theology and comparative religion studies, and he was the head of the psychology department at Fordham University. Although he had never been on television, he was an accomplished public speaker. The current controversy held particular interest for him since his mother's side of the family was unusually insightful, and many of his relatives had participated in extrasensory perception experiments. Consequently, he had been hearing about telepathy his entire life and had written books about psychic phenomena.

Father McCarthy turned to thank his host and then looked directly at the camera as he started his remarks. "I'm here this evening to address my concerns regarding the unfortunate on-air comments from a Florida priest about one of his teenage parishioners earlier today. I want to preface my statement by saying that neither Father Sullivan nor myself speak for the Catholic Church. We are simply two individuals trying to do the right thing."

Father McCarthy ran his hand over his bald head and paused for a moment before continuing. "Throughout history, individuals have described wondrous events that occurred when their hearts stopped beating. Often, these near-death experiences changed the course of their lives. It appears that we are witnessing such a change in three Fort Lauderdale teenagers who claim to have experienced a feeling of connectedness with the Universe during their individual near-death experiences. These teens want to use this principle of connectivity among people to try to bring peace to the world."

He leaned forward in his chair and challenged the viewers. "I say let them try. There's no magic involved or demonic possession. Extrasensory perception has played an important role in religious and self-enlightenment practices for centuries. It is alive and well in Charismatic Catholicism, Kabbalah Judaism, Zen

Buddhism, India, and throughout Central and South America."

The priest took a sip of water and leaned back in his chair. "This is not an attempt to undermine anyone's religious beliefs. The kids took a look at the world and decided they wanted an alternative approach to prayer. Now, those of us who spend long hours praying may not agree with this, but there's no need for us to feel threatened by it either. If they believe that sending images of peace out into a soup of consciousness will make the world a less violent place, so be it. If it works, we can have a thoughtful and rational discussion on the science behind it. If it doesn't work, they've done no harm. Their cause is an honorable one."

He crossed his legs and rubbed the side of his face before he began speaking again. "I believe Father Sullivan chose his words carelessly without realizing his implied threat of violence. I also believe that he owes Annie McDoogan and her colleagues a public apology."

Father Sullivan sat alone in his Manhattan hotel room, listening to the broadcasts. As he reached for the remote, chest pains hit him like a hammer. With his heart pounding, he took the ever-present bottle of baby aspirin from his pocket and swallowed a tablet.

I will not stop. Annie's soul must be saved. She's the closest thing that I'll ever have to a daughter, and I need to help her. I miss Colleen's companionship. Why can't things just go back to the way they were before the shark attack? Oh, God help me!

Chapter 15

Annie was dismayed over the painting on the church. Her family had always been close to Father Sullivan, and she felt it wasn't fair to depict him as a devil. She didn't want her crusade turning into a conflict about good versus evil. She was trying to help people, and all of this was an unnecessary distraction.

Ming and Emir, however, had a different opinion. Ming felt that any publicity advanced their cause and gained supporters. Emir thought the drawing was epic and had the picture blown up to poster size. He printed three copies and made a show of presenting them to the girls. Annie rolled hers up and put it in the closet, but Ming and Emir hung theirs in their bedrooms. It made them laugh to see Annie as an angel.

The protest at the church may have been disrupted the previous night, but emotions were still running high on Thursday morning. Some of the kids from the parish started going door-to-door selling T-shirts imprinted with the infamous picture and encouraging the younger members of the households to wear the shirts to the next 10 a.m. Sunday Mass.

Word started to spread that something big was going to happen on Sunday. Activists on both sides of the issue lit up the Internet with calls to action. Something was brewing, and supporters and opponents started to prepare for the impending fireworks. Some organizers arranged caravans to transport like-minded individuals from other counties to the church.

Annie caught wind of it and posted a plea for calm on their website. She took to social media and reached out to her supporters and begged them to remember that this was a peace movement. She wanted no violence and couldn't bear the thought that someone would be injured on her account. Her requests were ignored.

Everything was spinning out of control, and Annie felt lost and alone. She slipped into a deep depression and suffered from a feeling of foreboding that she couldn't shake. She wouldn't eat, and stopped answering the phone and replying to emails. She retreated from the world and stayed in her bed for hours at a time. Colleen called Dr. Lamberti, who agreed to come over to the house at noon the next day if Annie was still unresponsive.

Annie was having trouble distinguishing dreams from reality and experienced no surprise when her father appeared. She was neither happy nor sad to see him.

Hi, Daddy.
Hello, pumpkin. Why so sad?
Life sucks.
Annie, you have work to do.

I don't care.

You must care. It's important.

Go away, Daddy. I've had enough.

"Annie. Annie, wake up." Dr. Lamberti bent over the bed and gently shook Annie's shoulder. "Wake up. It's Friday afternoon."

Annie groaned. "Go away. I don't want to talk to anybody." She pulled the covers over her head and curled into a tight ball.

"Annie, we need to talk."

She sat up and pulled the covers down to her chest. "What?"

Dr. Lamberti sat at the foot of the bed facing her young patient. "How do you feel?"

Annie threw her extra pillow on the floor. "Lousy. Something bad is going to happen, and it's going to be all my fault."

"And you think staying in bed is going to help?"

"It helps me! I can't deal with this anymore." Annie pulled her knees up to her chest and started sobbing.

The doctor was relieved to see the tears. It was better than withdrawing into a shell and not reacting to anything. "Annie, I'm going to give your mother a prescription for some medicine that I think will make you feel better. I'm also going to have your mother make an appointment for you to have some tests run at the hospital."

Annie wiped her nose on her sheets. "What kind of tests?"

Dr. Lamberti smiled as she started to see the old Annie peeking through. "Well, since the shark attack, you've been experiencing a lot of mood swings. I want to make sure that there isn't something physically wrong with you that we might be able to fix."

"Okay... "

"First, they'll do a brain scan to see if the drowning or seizures caused any damage that we can see. Then, you'll have some blood drawn and pee in a cup. Okay?"

"Okay. Thanks, doc."

"Welcome back, Annie. Now go eat some lunch."

The pills did the trick, and Annie felt much better by suppertime. In fact, she felt so good that she began planning a joint birthday party for Ming and herself. They both turned 16 next week, and Annie felt like celebrating. Ming agreed, and they decided to have it on Tuesday night. Emir was happy to come, so all three sets of parents were invited to dinner at Annie's house, and the kids would go to a late movie afterward. The parents had never met each other, and everyone thought it was a good idea to get together since the teenagers were becoming such good friends.

Annie slept well that night without giving Sunday's services a second thought. That would soon change.

Chapter 16

Emir was not involved in organizing the Sunday protest, but he was determined to confront the priest and demand an apology for his careless remarks. Consequently, he arrived early at the church and secured a front-row seat. It was his first time in a Catholic church, and he wasn't entirely comfortable. He turned in his seat to watch the crowd filing in and was pleasantly surprised to see the majority of teenagers wearing Annie's T-shirt. It made him feel proud to be part of the group. A few girls immediately recognized him and hurried to grab a seat near the superstar. Emir took it in stride and impatiently waited for the Mass to begin.

Father Sullivan had been warned ahead of time to expect a large turnout, so he wasn't surprised to see people standing in the side aisles. However, the sea of white T-shirts with his face on the body of a devil caused him to stumble and momentarily consider canceling the service. But, he was here to do God's work, and a bunch of insubordinate kids wasn't going to stop him. He decided to carry on and hold his comments for the sermon.

Mass was uneventful until the priest stepped up to the pulpit to begin his sermon. Electricity pulsed through the crowd as they waited to hear the tone of his words. Father Sullivan felt the tension but chose to stick to his planned remarks. He looked straight at Emir as he began speaking.

"Welcome to all the first-time visitors. I can tell by your fashion statements that many of you are upset with me, and I'm sorry for that. However, as your spiritual leader, it's my duty to do what I feel is proper, and right now I feel that this so-called peace movement is an abomination against God."

Emir jumped to his feet and raised his right hand with his index and middle fingers forming the letter V. Another teen joined him, then another, until the momentum spread and half the church was standing.

Suddenly, Emir began to sing Ming's song. More and more voices joined in until the church swelled with the sound of the peace anthem. The organist began accompanying them, and the song became a true celebration of unity.

Emir was so caught up in the emotion of the moment that he moved to the center aisle and began waving his hands as if he were a maestro conducting his orchestra. It was a totally spontaneous action, and he felt joyful. For the first time in his life, he felt that he had a purpose. He wasn't just his parents' son. He was more than a pampered rich boy. He could be a leader!

Father Sullivan returned to the altar and continued the Mass in silence. He skipped the distribution of communion wafers and allowed his congregation to continue to vent their disappointment with him. He left the altar and returned to the rectory.

Without the priest there to fuel their anger, the singing soon tapered off, and people began to leave. When Emir reached the yard, a disheveled man in jeans blocked his way. He was a few inches shorter than Emir and a few years older with greasy hair and chewing tobacco juice dribbling from the corner of his mouth.

"Hey, rag head, why don't you go back where you belong?"

Emir stiffened. He didn't hear these types of slurs very often. "Are you talking to me?"

The man took another step closer. "You see any other Arabs around here?"

"Born in New York, buddy. I'm as American as you are."

"You and your friends better stop this mind-control business, or you'll be sorry." He poked Emir in the chest as he spoke.

Emir stepped back and crouched slightly. "I'm only going to tell you this once, pal. You touch me again, and you'll be on the ground in two seconds."

"You're the big man, huh?"

"I don't want to fight you, but if I have to, I will. Now, get out of here and cool off."

The man turned to leave but then came back and spat tobacco juice two inches from Emir's foot. "Nobody's got the right to mess with my mind. You're going to regret this. I've got my eye on ugly Annie."

Emir's foot shot out, hooked the man's ankle, and he was sprawled out on the ground before he knew what was happening.

Somebody yelled, "Look out!"

Emir reacted instinctively as another shorter, heavier man grabbed him from behind. Emir flipped him over his head and hit him in the face while the man was struggling to his feet. Girls screamed as blood started spurting from the broken nose.

The two attackers were back on their feet and circling Emir. A couple of the boys in the crowd were running in to help him when the heavier man pulled a switchblade out of his pocket and warned the spectators to stay away.

The men began their synchronized attack from opposite directions. The shorter man approached from behind with his knife firmly grasped in his right hand. The taller man sneered as he slowly came forward. They were smiling as they forced Emir back toward the church wall.

Emir continued to circle so he could keep an eye on both of them and plan his defense. He could hear the sirens from the police cars, but he knew this would be over before the cops arrived. He bounced lightly on the soles of his feet as he assessed the situation and decided his first priority was to disable the knife-wielding man. He knew that his attack had to be perfectly timed if he was going to walk away without suffering a serious injury.

Both men slowly inched closer and closer. Emir could smell the alcohol on their breath mixed with old sweat. But, they weren't amateurs. They had been fighting dirty for a long time. The taller man reached down and grabbed a handful of soil from a flowerbed while the other man began tossing his knife back and forth between his hands.

Fsssh! The dirt hit Emir's eyes. *Swish!* The blade sliced through the air, just missing his chest. The adrenaline pounded through Emir's veins as he let his body react. He turned to face the knife. With one smooth movement, his left leg shot out and broke the heavier man's wrist, knocking the knife out of his hand. Without breaking his momentum, he spun around, and his right foot caught the taller man in the chest and sent him flying straight toward the arriving police cars. His broken ribs prevented any possibility of escape.

The crowd cheered as the police secured the scene and took statements from Emir and some of the onlookers. The two attackers were handcuffed and shoved into a police car. The taller man, who was sitting by the window, rapped on the glass to get Emir's attention. With eyes full of hate, he mouthed the words, "I know where Annie lives."

Chapter 17

The two attackers posted bail after doctors tended to their injuries. The Coral Springs police were warned to keep a lookout for the men's gray pickup truck around Ming's or Annie's house. Since Emir lived in a gated community, the license plate number and photographs of the two men were given to the security guards with instructions to call the Fort Lauderdale police if anyone spotted them within the community.

Emir was determined to keep Annie safe and persuaded her mother to invest in a security system. But, that wasn't enough to put his mind at ease. He spent many hours driving around her neighborhood, searching for any sign of trouble. The stress and lack of sleep started taking a toll on his body. His eyes darted at any unusual sound, and the dark circles under his eyes made him appear years older than his actual age.

Annie insisted on moving forward with her party planning, so Emir forced himself to focus on buying birthday presents for Ming and Annie. Ming was easy. He purchased two tickets for her to the next Broadway touring production at the Broward Center for the Performing Arts. He figured that she would take Annie, so the gift was actually a twofer. But, if Ming chose to go with somebody else, he wanted to give Annie her own gift. That was a harder decision. After a lengthy deliberation, he decided to buy her a pair of emerald earrings. He thought the vibrant green gems were the exact color of her eyes and would look great against her dark red hair.

Emir was glad that Annie had invited the parents to the party. He liked Annie's mother and thought his parents would too. He was looking forward to meeting Ming's family since their daughter was such a character. They must be very patient individuals.

Annie was feeling great. The attacker's comments at the church had hurt her feelings, but she was bursting with pride in the way Emir defended her. That initially left her with mixed feelings since she was leading a peace movement, but she got over it. After all, she was attacked, and he was just defending her. Perhaps a little too forcibly, but he was sticking up for *her*. Life couldn't get any better than this.

She decided that she was tired of the ugly duckling remarks. It was time for a change. So, Tuesday morning she walked over to the Coral Square Mall and, for the first time in her life, entered a beauty parlor. She told the hairdresser to pick a style, and he went to work on her long, stringy red hair. When he finished, she was the proud owner of a bouncy shoulder-length bob. Then, she went next door to Kohl's and bought some tops and a pair of jeans that showed off her curves. This was building up to be the best birthday ever.

The party was soon off to a great start. Annie received lots of compliments on her new hairdo, and an animated Emir recounted Sunday's events. Ming was thrilled that everyone knew the words to her song but was surprised to find that Emir could sing. She enjoyed putting him on the spot and after much prodding, he stood up and sang the first stanza of the song. The girls then jumped up and helped him finish it. The parents collapsed in laughter as they watched their offspring acting out in front of them. Their kids had definitely bonded, and they were thankful for it although none of them could rest easy when there was so much opposition.

The three friends went out to the backyard to play a quick game of croquet before the Chinese food arrived. High hedges surrounded the yard, so neighbors had no opportunity to spy on the infamous teenagers. Unfortunately, the shrubbery also prevented the kids from seeing the gray pickup as it drove slowly by the house.

Inside, the adults were getting to know each other. Daphne Polat was a beautiful woman who spoke in a soft, slightly accented voice.

"Emir is very fond of Annie and Ming. He has no sisters, so I think they are a good influence on him. What he's experiencing now will help him later when he becomes a doctor and marries a good Muslim woman."

Her equally good-looking husband, Mehmet, agreed. "Yes, both girls seem well grounded and are working together to make society better for everyone. I admire that. Just like your husband, Colleen. Emir told us he was killed while building a school in Afghanistan. He must have been a very good man."

Colleen smiled slightly. "Yes, he was, and we miss him terribly. But, life goes on, and Annie seems like she is finally recovering. She's going back to school in September and will be sharing some classes with Ming. She's happier today than she's been in a long while."

Lilly Chang poured herself a glass of wine. "Annie's helped Ming focus on a goal and work hard to make it succeed. That's something her father and I have never been able to do."

Zhong chuckled at the thought of his scatterbrained daughter. "She's always wanted to live her life in the spotlight. We never thought it would start this early. She's very proud that the video of her singing and being shot has more than one million YouTube views." He shook his head in amazement. "I wish as many people were interested in my piano concerts."

Lilly chimed in. "Or my art."

Colleen turned toward Emir's parents. "Your son was a true hero that day. I will always be grateful that he tried to protect Annie."

Lilly nodded. "Yes, I still cry when I see the video of him picking Ming up so gently. You have a remarkable boy."

Colleen's eyes teared up. "I think we're all thankful they found each other. No matter what the future brings, may God keep them safe."

Dinner was a lively affair with everyone passing the cartons of food around the table. By the time Colleen brought out the ice cream cake, sounds of laughter filled the home. Ming was doing impressions of her favorite actors, and she showed a real talent for accents.

Annie suddenly stopped laughing. "Hey, Mom. Is something burning in the kitchen?"

At the next moment, Emir noticed black smoke curling out from Annie's bedroom. "Fire! Annie's room is on fire!"

Suddenly, Ming cried out. "It's not just Annie's room! The whole back of the house is on fire! We have to get out! Somebody call 911."

Zhong grabbed Colleen's keys by the door and rushed to move her car out of the garage. "Do you have a hose?"

Colleen yelled back. "In the garage."

Mehmet ran after Zhong, found the hose and went searching for the outside faucet. Ming ignored what everybody else was doing and grabbed all the birthday presents and piled them in a heap across the street.

Annie ran to her room and pulled open the door. *Whoosh!* A wall of heat and smoke hit her like a hammer. "I have to get in."

Colleen screamed. "Annie, shut the door. You're spreading the fire!"

"No, I have to get daddy's stuff out of my closet." Annie put her hands over her face and ran into the room.

Emir was two seconds behind her. "Annie!" The others could hear their strangled coughs and muffled cries.

Annie kept moving toward the closet. "I have to get his things. They're all I've got left!" Emir caught her arm. She tried to shake him loose. "Let me go!"

He grabbed her around the waist. "Let's go."

Annie pulled hard against his grasp. "You're hurting me!"

Emir swiped at the cinders in her hair and threw her over his shoulder. "We don't have time!"

She beat her fists against his back to no avail. He was a man on a mission, and that mission was to get her to safety. He was vaguely aware of the chaos as he ran out of the house and dropped her spitting and hissing on the lawn across the street. He grabbed her again as she started to run back to the burning house.

"Are you trying to kill yourself? Sit down and shut up, or I'll sit on you." Emir was quickly losing his temper.

Annie glared at him and then sat down. Colleen reached her and pulled her into her arms, gently rocking her baby girl.

"Oh, honey. I'm so sorry. We lost dad's clothes and letters, but he'll always be in our hearts."

Annie's only reply was a low, painful moan. Colleen kept rocking her slowly back and forth. Mehmet was spraying the house when the fire engines pulled up. Daphne and Lilly tried to move what they could out of the kitchen and living room. Colleen asked them to retrieve the photo albums that were in an end-table drawer. Those were her most precious possessions.

Annie started to cry. "Mommy, what are we going to do now?"

Chapter 18

The fire inspector told Colleen that someone had cut through the windows and screens and thrown Molotov cocktails into the three back rooms. The accelerant caused the fire to burn fast and hot. The walls were cement and survived the damage, but the contents were destroyed. Colleen called her landlord with the news and took photos of the damage in order to collect on her renter's insurance. For the time being, she and Annie had no place to stay and no clothes except what they were wearing. But, she had her credit cards and started looking up hotel rates on her phone. At least it was summertime when the rooms were the cheapest. Thank God for small blessings.

Daphne walked over and sat down next to Colleen. "I hope they catch whoever did this."

Colleen nodded. "A friend of mine is a security expert, and after Emir was attacked, I asked him to put cameras in the trees around the house. He checked the video feed, and it clearly shows the same two men that threatened Emir. So, the police will catch them and have enough evidence to put them away for a long time. The kids will be safe." She wiped some soot from her eyes. "Oh, I still haven't thanked Emir for protecting Annie once again. I'm beginning to think he's her guardian angel."

Daphne smiled. "The job suits him. It's heartwarming to see him care so much about other people." She paused for a moment. "Speaking of caring, we want you and Annie to come stay with us for a while."

Colleen started to shake her head, but Daphne stopped her. "We have two extra bedrooms. My parents and in-laws visit every other summer, but this is the off year. Really, this is something we would like to do. I'm going to invite Ming as well."

"Did I hear my name?" Ming walked over and stood in front of them.

Daphne looked up. "Would you like to come stay with us until the police catch the men who did this? We live in a very secure gated community, and you can share a room with Annie."

Ming's face lit up. "Hey, Emir! Annie and I are going to come live with you."

"Hey, girlfriend. Wake up." Ming bounced up and down on Annie's bed. "It's morning."

Annie opened one eye. "When did you get here?"

Ming grinned. "Just arrived." She pointed to some clothes hanging in the closet. "I brought you a few things that might fit. My mom's about your size, and she donated some slacks, tops, nightgowns and a robe.

Your mom's going to take you over to the mall later today to buy more stuff."

Annie sat up. "Yeah, like bras and underwear. I don't want to wear anybody's used lingerie."

Ming grimaced. "Eew. That's gross. Come on, roomie. Get up and get some breakfast." She threw the extra pillow at her. "I'll be in the kitchen with Emir."

Annie stayed in bed a few moments longer, thinking about last night's fire. When she finally got up, her lips were set in a thin, determined line. She needed to have a serious talk with Emir and Ming. She walked over to the closet to see what Ming had brought and noticed her clothes from last night had been washed and stacked on top of the dresser. She'd have to remember to thank her mother. The thought of her mom made her hurry, and she soon made her appearance in the kitchen.

Her mother, Emir and Ming were sitting at the kitchen table eating some fruit when Annie interrupted them. "Morning, all."

"Annie! How are you feeling, honey?" Colleen quickly assessed her daughter's mental and physical condition. "You look like you slept well."

"Yup, great mattress. Hi, Emir. Thanks for having us."

Emir smiled. "Thank my parents. I wouldn't have thought of it. But, I'm glad you're here where you'll be safe." He looked like he had finally gotten a solid night's sleep.

Annie grabbed a cereal bowl and helped herself to some sliced mixed fruit. As she ate, she walked around inspecting her new residence. She particularly liked the modern art. Colorful paintings were everywhere and brightened up the pure white walls. The dark hardware floors contrasted nicely with the pale walls and gleamed in the bright sunlight that poured in through the Florida room windows. Annie could see a yard full of flowering shrubs as she walked outside to the pool.

The pool itself was gorgeous with plenty of room for Emir to swim his laps when he was in training. One end featured a sparkling waterfall while an inviting hot tub held the place of honor at the opposite end. A tear started to run down Annie's cheek as she looked at the peaceful scene.

Emir came up beside her with a worried look on his face. "What's wrong? Don't you like it?"

Annie looked down, so he wouldn't see her crying. "Daddy would have loved this." Her voice broke as she continued. "Now, I have nothing left of his."

Emir reached down in his pocket. "Not quite." He pulled out a handful of brass buttons and medals and placed them in Annie's hand. "I went over to your house this morning and dug through the ashes. I think these are from your father's uniform."

Annie gave a squeal of joy and threw her arms around Emir. "Oh, thank you."

Ming shouted from the kitchen. "Hey, you two. What's going on?"

Annie gave him one last squeeze before they laughed and walked back inside. Annie showed the treasure to her mother, kissed her on the cheek and sat down next to her. "I'm sorry for all the trouble I've caused you."

Colleen put her arm around her daughter's shoulder. "Honey, we need to talk about what happened. You have to stop. This is getting too dangerous, and the next time someone may be killed."

Annie pulled away and saw that her friends' expressions mirrored her own. The joyful moment ended. She had expected this reaction from her mother, and it was time to take a stand. "This is Father John's fault. He's the one who inflames the fanatics and wackos. We're going after him."

Emir pushed his chair away from the table. "I'm sorry, Mrs. McDoogan. My parents also told me to quit. But, it's not going to happen. What we're trying to do is too important. It's revolutionary!" He stood up and started pacing. "The violence in our society is out of control, and we think we may have a solution." He scratched his chin. "Or at least part of the solution. We won't know if it's working until we see crime statistics go down in our cities, and the terrorists cease their brutality."

Ming leaned forward in her chair. "Even then, we probably won't get any credit for the changes. But, it doesn't matter. We're doing it because it's the right thing to do."

Annie looked at her mother. "Father John is hurting us, and we're going to take him down."

Emir frowned as he remembered the psychic's warning of danger. He spoke his next words in an authoritative tone that allowed no objections, even from Colleen. "You're all going to take a self-defense class from my martial arts instructor. Even my parents and Ming's agreed to participate. It'll be fun. He's coming over on Saturday morning at 10:00. Wear comfortable clothes."

Frank Peterson arrived exactly at 10, carrying a large duffel bag full of padding to the back yard. He was a young, attractive and very fit man, and Annie and Ming were immediately distracted. Frank sensed this and quickly got down to business. The first exercise was designed to help potential victims lose their inhibitions and scream if they felt threatened. Ming was a natural at this since she treated it as an acting lesson. It took the others some time to scream loud enough to meet Frank's approval.

For the next exercise, the group worked in pairs: Emir's parents, Ming's parents, Annie and Colleen, and Ming and Emir. The goal was to turn the tables on an attacker who had you pinned to the ground. Emir and Frank demonstrated how to reverse the position and mount the attacker. Everybody enjoyed this, especially Ming, who just lay there, grinning up at Emir when he pinned her. Her father saw what was going on and quickly switched places with Emir. Ming pouted for a minute but ended up having fun wrestling with her dad.

The next skill made the men cringe but was directed at the females. Frank put on his padding, and Emir demonstrated how to knee and kick a male attacker in the groin. The females were remarkably reluctant to use any force until Frank started taunting and threatening them. Once they were angry, they dropped their inhibitions and let him have it. When it was over, Daphne and Lilly collapsed in exhaustion, feeling a surprising sense of satisfaction. Their husbands would never look at them in quite the same way again.

During the break, Annie asked Frank if he could teach them to kick like Emir did when he was under attack at the church. He smiled and told her that took years of training, but he could show them the basics. So, for the next set of drills, he removed his pads and worked with Emir to demonstrate the moves in slow motion. Then, he put on his pads and face mask and invited Annie to come up front. He put her through the paces and let her continue to practice with him until she was comfortable. He and Emir then worked with the others, stressing that they put the whole force of their body behind their kicks.

The last topic that he covered was how to use everyday materials as weapons. He looked around the yard and pointed out the pottery, landscaping stones and patio furniture. When he was done, everyone clapped and thanked him for the instruction.

Annie felt much more confident. *Now, I'm ready for anything.*

Chapter 19

While Colleen was out running errands, and Emir's parents were busy seeing patients, the three crusaders decided to take advantage of the quiet and work on planning their strategy to neutralize Father Sullivan. Emir grabbed a notebook and pen and started the discussion.

"One way or another, we have to silence this guy. The way I see it, we convince someone in the Church to order him to stop his remarks, or we build up public pressure to the point where he throws in the towel and surrenders."

Annie frowned. "He thinks he's on a religious quest, so I don't think pressure will make a difference. He's committed to his cause."

Ming started waving her hands. "We launch a publicity campaign against him so that the Church has to act. Maddie Greenwald's coming Saturday to do another magazine interview, so we can ask her for help. And we can ask the Jesuit priest who defended us on

TV to intercede. Maybe he has some connections that can help us. This will be epic!"

Emir scratched his cheek and reached for his coffee cup. "I can put the contact info for his bishop and cardinal on our website and encourage people to write letters asking them to stop him from endangering kids' lives."

Annie took a bite of her donut as she considered other possibilities. "Ming, when does your song hit the airwaves?"

Ming's face brightened. "The group called me yesterday and said it's going to drop next week." She jumped up. "I forgot to tell you! They said they wanted to record an album of peace songs if I would write them!"

Annie threw her arms in the air. "That's fantastic! Music can be a very powerful way to reach people! Maybe you can include some kind of reference to what Father John's doing."

Emir smiled. "You'll have to sit still long enough to write the songs."

"No problem, big boy. But, you'll have to put up with my guitar playing."

Emir looked around the room and pointed toward the back wall. "Nobody uses the study much. You can always go in there and shut the door."

Ming reached for a mango. "Thanks." She took a bite of the juicy fruit. "Hey, Annie, why don't we try a little of our own mind control on Father Sullivan?"

Annie shook her head. "The kids in the parish already tried that. It doesn't seem to be working."

Emir was out of ideas, so he walked over to the Florida room, reached down and took a wrapped present and an envelope off a table. "You two haven't opened my birthday presents." He gave the package to Annie. "You first."

"Oh, I almost forget about the presents." She tore off the wrapping paper and squealed in delight. "Earrings! They're beautiful! Thank you."

Emir's face burst into a relieved grin. "I'm glad you like them. They match your eyes."

Annie blushed and looked down at the floor. "I don't think my eyes shine like these jewels."

Emir murmured, "You need to look in the mirror sometime."

Ming didn't care for the tone of that conversation and grabbed the envelope out of his hand. "What did I get?" She screeched when she opened it. "Two tickets to a Broadway show!"

Emir shook his head slightly as Annie's mouth flew open. "Broadway road show in Fort Lauderdale, not New York."

Ming looked up at Emir. "You want to go with me?"

Emir looked down at her hopeful face. "No, I go to the mosque on Friday nights."

Ming stomped her foot. "That's no excuse. I'll exchange the tickets for another night or matinee."

Emir sighed. "No, Muslims aren't allowed to go on dates alone. We can go out in groups, but not alone."

Ming's eyebrows shot up. "Then, I'll get two more tickets, and one of your friends can take Annie."

Hey! Annie threw the rest of her donut at Ming. "No! You're not pimping me out." There was no way she would help Ming date Emir.

Ming laughed. "All right. You want to go with me instead?"

Annie smiled. "You've got a date. Now, let's get to work on Father Sullivan."

Strangely enough, Ming got a call later that day from a high school buddy asking her out for a movie on Friday night. He said his 16-year-old cousin was in town and would like to double date with Annie if she was free. Ming pretended to ask Annie and then told Jack that they would be ready Friday night at 7:00.

Annie walked in the bedroom as Ming was hanging up. "Sorry, but I couldn't help overhearing. Who are you going to see Friday night?"

Ming grinned. "*We* are going to the movies with two boys."

"What are you talking about?"

"Well, Emir's not going to date us, so when a friend from school called, I said yes."

Annie frowned. "But nobody asked *me*."

"Jack is cute, and I've wanted to date him for ages. I don't think he'd go unless his cousin could come along. You don't really mind, do you?"

Annie sat down on her bed. Her expression was a mixture of sadness and excitement. "I've never been on a date. I'll have to ask my mom."

Ming threw her pillow in the air. "Hurray! We'll have a blast!"

Date night arrived, and the girls were ready and waiting. Emir had been acting weird all week after hearing the news and was at the mosque for prayers when the boys arrived to pick up their dates. Annie and Ming wore jeans and carried sweaters in case the theater's air conditioning was too cold for them. Jack introduced his cousin, Tom, and they were on their way. Jack was good-looking with an athletic build, but Annie preferred Tom. It was like looking in a mirror. He had red hair and freckles and showed up wearing an Albert Einstein T-shirt. Annie was delighted and instantly felt comfortable with him. He admitted that he wore it after reading about Annie online, but it *was* his.

Once inside the theater, however, she got a little nervous as the lights went out, and the movie started. Tom put his arm around her in the dark, and she didn't know what to do. Was she supposed to snuggle up against him or reach up and hold the hand draped over her shoulder? Looking at Ming was no help because she had thrown her sweater over Jack's head and was busy getting better acquainted. Annie clutched her sweater that was lying in her lap and sat up straight in her seat staring at the screen. Tom sensed her discomfort and left to buy some popcorn. When he got back, sharing the box gave them something to do, and they both relaxed and enjoyed the movie.

Outside the theater, Ming told Annie to go ahead to the restaurant next door, and she and Jack would meet them there in a little bit. Annie wanted to argue, but Ming had already skipped off and was walking away toward Jack's car. So, she shrugged it off and walked over to the restaurant with Tom and ordered some appetizers.

The night turned out to be a lot of fun for Annie. Tom enjoyed physics as much as she did, and they had a great time discussing her spider-web-energy-matrix theory. He liked her idea of connections between people and wanted to know more about her after-life experience when she met her dad. He was fascinated, and they were both disappointed when Ming and Jack showed up 45 minutes later.

Tom was only in town for a few more days and, at the front door, asked Annie to go to the planetarium in Davie with him on Saturday night. She readily agreed and smiled up at him. He took that as a good sign, put one hand along the back of her neck, slowly leaned over, closed his eyes and kissed her goodnight. Her brain exploded at the sensation. His lips were so soft, and her skin was tingling. She had never felt anything like this. She liked being kissed!

Annie wouldn't have felt quite so joyful if she had noticed Emir, sitting in the dark, watching her from between the slats of the venetian blinds in his bedroom window. His night had not gone well. At the social meeting after prayers, he had found himself searching the covered heads for a green-eyed, freckled-face girl.

Chapter 20

Maddie Greenwald arrived at Emir's house on Saturday morning along with Paul, her photographer, who applied makeup to the girls. Emir looked tired, and Paul tried to talk him into wearing some concealer under his eyes, but he refused. So, Paul took the photos and left. Annie was glad that she could wear jeans this time and that no more close-ups of her scar were required. She was also relieved that the adults were out of the house, so the kids would feel free to say whatever was on their minds. Annie noticed that Maddie was now a blond and wearing eyeliner and mascara. She looked much younger. Things must be going well for her.

After some initial chitchat, Maddie turned on her tape recorder and said with a smile, "Let's get started. I have some good news for you. Annie's article generated so much publicity that our international editors have agreed to simultaneously publish this interview on the same day as the North American release. Be prepared for an immediate worldwide response, both positive and negative."

Ming shouted, "We're ready!"

Maddie continued. "The first article was split 50/50 between favorable and unfavorable opinions. As you might expect, the Asian countries accepted the idea of telepathy much more readily than the western world. We'll see what happens this time."

The kids looked apprehensively at each other as Maddie made a few notes on her pad. "It's been a few weeks since I wrote the first article, so I need to catch my readers up on what's going on with you three. One of you want to tell me what happened in New York?"

Emir wanted revenge and spoke first. "Father Sullivan brought the protesters with him from Florida in order to start the riot. He wants national attention, and we're his means to an end."

Annie interrupted him. "That's not completely fair. He honestly believes I'm possessed by the devil."

Emir shot back. "You're being used, whether he's aware of it or not. He desperately wants to feel relevant and be in the spotlight. The priest's behavior was irresponsible, and somebody could have been seriously hurt. Now, he's telling people to stop us any way they can."

"Hang on a minute." Ming ran to her room and returned with her T-shirt of angelic Annie facing the satanic priest.

Maddie laughed and took some photos of the shirt. "That would certainly upset him."

Annie continued the story. "Apparently, it did. Emir went to Mass the next Sunday, and Father Sullivan said our movement was an abomination."

Ming couldn't contain her pride. "Emir stood up and started singing my song, and half the church joined in! So cool."

Emir frowned. "Yeah, right up to the moment somebody attacked me."

Maddie was startled. "You were attacked in church?"

Emir scratched his chin. "Not exactly, two rednecks jumped me outside on the lawn. They're out on bail right now."

Annie started wringing her hands. "And they tried to burn down my house Tuesday night. They were caught on camera. I'll email you a copy of the video."

Emir continued. "Now, you know everything. Annie, her mother and Ming are living here until the men are sitting in jail."

Ming hung her head and spoke in a low voice. "My parents didn't want to come. They said our address was unpublished, and they didn't want to leave the house. I'm worried about them."

Maddie made a few notes. "Okay. How can I help?"

Ming looked straight at Maddie. "The priest should be suspended. Your readers need to complain to his bishop and cardinal. His words are putting our lives in danger."

Maddie liked this girl with the spiky hair. "How has this experience changed you?"

"Parts of it have been amazing! I get love letters from around the world, and now I'm a songwriter."

Maddie shook her head. "Yes, but you've also been shot, and all your mail can't be full of compliments."

Ming frowned. "All of us get hate mail, but we wouldn't change places with anybody. We want to change the world. How many kids can say that?"

Annie and Emir nodded in agreement as Maddie continued to look at Ming. "Father Sullivan accused this group of trying to turn people away from God. As a Buddhist, how do you reply?"

Ming sighed. "Well, we don't really believe in a god. Buddhists think that religions have gods so that people will fear the consequences of bad deeds. Buddhism is more about compassion, enlightenment and feeling connected with the rest of the Universe."

Maddie wasn't ready to drop the subject. "So, this experience hasn't changed your religious views?"

Ming looked down at the floor before answering. "I didn't say that. Dying and being in touch with other survivors changed me. I no longer believe in reincarnation, which is a focal point in the Buddhist religion. They believe people are reborn until they gain true enlightenment. I no longer think that's possible, so I suppose I'm no longer a real Buddhist. But, I'll always revere the Dalai Lama. He's a wonderful man."

Maddie looked up from her notes. "How do you explain people remembering past lives?"

Ming rubbed her nose. "I think that they are unknowingly receiving communications from someone who has died."

Maddie scribbled on her pad for a few moments. "What specifically caused you to change your beliefs?"

Ming shrugged. "Annie and Emir saw dead relatives. The idea that their unique essences would be transported into other beings, maybe even a cockroach, is horrifying to me now."

Maddie nodded that she understood. "Emir, what about you? Has your experience changed any of your Islamic beliefs?"

Emir exhaled forcibly. He hadn't expected this question. "Well, Muslims believe that angels remove your spirit when you die and escort you to heaven for a brief moment. I don't have a problem with that."

He ran his fingers through his hair. "However, I don't believe that you're then returned to earth, and your soul is held in storage as you sleep until Judgment Day." He sighed. "But, I'm not a scholar, and I don't sit around with my Muslim friends talking about death. We talk sports."

He smiled. "I do know that all three of us touched an unimaginably vibrant consciousness, comprised of an almost infinite number of beings." He paused for a moment. "Maybe scholars would interpret this as meaning that the invisible community includes everyone except the Muslims who are sleeping. But, I saw my aunt, so now... "

Emir stood up and started to pace. "It doesn't matter to me. There are parts of my religion that are beautiful. True Muslims dedicate themselves to helping the poor and building strong families and communities. The quality of your life affects your afterlife. They value education. So, yes, I have differences, but I am proud to call myself a Muslim."

He continued to pace as Maddie took notes. The interview continued for about ten more minutes and ended with Maddie agreeing to print the contact information for Father Sullivan's superiors. She also agreed to include Ming's request for movie and television executives to embed subliminal messages of peace in their productions.

Maddie was happy with the interview and was certain a group photo of the photogenic teens would attract readers to the magazine. The editors were going to rush the article into publication next week. The kids were a hot ticket, and there was no time to lose. Her final thoughts were more personal and selfish. *The reincarnation and soul-storage remarks will cause a backlash. Keep stirring the pot, Maddie, and ride their coattails all the way to a Pulitzer.*

Chapter 21

The word went out for kids to show up early for Sunday Mass and fill all the pews except for the first and last rows. These were reserved for special attendees including Annie, Ming and Emir, who sat in the back. Like most of the other teenagers in attendance, they were wearing the Annie-angel T-shirt that had quickly become the favorite shirt for kids around the world.

Ming coordinated the day's activities. It was her job to contact the local supporters and give a heads-up to a reporter who came to the Mass, accompanied by a cameraman. Ming hoped her strategy to catch the bishop's attention would work.

The first half of the service progressed without incident, and Father Sullivan breathed a sigh of relief. A voice in his head told him to skip the sermon, but he paid no attention. He had spied Annie and her friends and couldn't help himself from reaching out to them. "Satan's influence is on the rise throughout the world. Look at the violence around you, and the pure evil that's behind it. Innocents are being slaughtered in the name of God. This has to change! Don't allow yourselves to believe that God can't help. The devil works in mysterious ways and uses unsuspecting victims to do his work. It's not their fault, but they have to rid themselves of this terrible evil! Annie McDoogan, I call on you now to come forward and allow me to lay my hands on you and cast out this demon!"

Annie stood up and made her way to the center aisle. Father Sullivan began trembling with anticipation. "Come, my child. Everyone can see how much you've changed. Let me help you find your way back."

His joy was short-lived as Emir and Ming got up and stood on either side of her. As they linked arms, the rest of the two back rows left their pews and stood in formation behind them. The group moved slowly toward the altar.

As they marched forward, the boys in the left front row entered the center aisle and approached the altar. Father Sullivan was speechless as the athletic teens encircled the pulpit, locking arms as they loomed over the shorter trapped priest. The tallest of the group assumed the position in front of the pulpit so that he hid the priest from view. Another boy disconnected his microphone.

As the procession reached the front of the church, Annie, Emir and Ming walked up the steps leading to the altar. Annie stood facing the congregation with her back touching the altar while Emir and Ming flanked her on a lower step. The remainder of the procession fanned out in front of the communion rail. Annie cleared her throat and began to speak.

"First, I'd like to thank Father Sullivan for the chance to speak during his sermon." She smiled as the cheers and laughter drowned out the muffled shouts coming from behind the pulpit. "He's right to think that I've changed. I may not be an angel..." She paused to point to her T-shirt angel and again waited for the laughter to subside. Her voice was stronger now as she gained confidence. "But, I have glimpsed heaven, and I'm here to tell you that it's indescribably beautiful and overflowing with a love that totally fills your senses. When you're there, you can feel the connection with an enormous number of souls."

The kids were hanging on every word, and the church was completely silent. "I think the power to connect with living beings lies within all of us, and I want to use this power to change the world!" The kids went crazy with shouts and cheers following this proclamation. "Are you with me?"

The crowd roared its agreement as Annie walked down the stairs and stood between Emir and Ming. They raised their joined hands high in the air. Annie was jubilant. "Send out your images of peace. They will be received! We will make the world a better place!"

Annie's voice started to shake as she spoke. "Because of Father Sullivan's words, we've been shot at, attacked and firebombed." She looked straight into the camera. "Father Sullivan wants to hurt us. Father Sullivan must go."

The church rocked with the rhythm of hundreds of voices chanting, "Father Sullivan must go" as the trio led the way down the aisle. Halfway out, they started to sing Ming's song, and the church filled with the sound of young voices singing their anthem. The boys guarding the pulpit left, and Father Sullivan forlornly watched as his church quickly emptied.

Annie was delighted to see Tom leaving the church. She had told him about her plans last night, but she had no idea that he was going to be here.

He walked over and kissed her cheek. "You're amazing!"

Annie felt her face getting warm and downplayed her role. "It's easy to get caught up in the moment. I couldn't have done it unless Emir and Ming were beside me."

"Do you want to go hang out? Maybe we can find a place that serves a decent brunch."

"Sounds good to me. Let's go." She turned and waved goodbye to Ming and Emir and took Tom's hand as they walked to his car.

Emir's eyes narrowed as he watched them leave. "Ming, how did their date go last night?"

"They went to the Sky show at the planetarium and got to use the telescope in the observatory. Annie said that when the observatory closed, they stretched out on the hood of Tom's car and tried to find the constellations featured in the show. She had a good time." She pushed him. "Where were you when he picked her up? I thought you'd be there."

"I had a tennis game." *And then I went to Davie, hid in the bushes and spied on Annie.*

Ming looked up at him. "You don't look so good. Are you having trouble sleeping?"

He straightened his shoulders. "I'm fine."

Ming noticed he didn't seem as well put together as usual. "Tuck in your shirt. You're a mess."

He did as she suggested. "Well, we might as well go home. I thought the three of us were going to go out and celebrate, but it looks like that's not going to happen."

"Cheer up. Annie will soon be back to normal. Tom's going back to Ohio on Tuesday." She didn't notice Emir's brightening expression. "But, she told me he's planning to come back next summer for 10 weeks."

Her words cut through him like a hot knife. Why was this happening to him? He wasn't an emotional guy. "Great."

Ming missed the sarcasm in his voice. "This won't last. They're too much alike. Annie needs someone who'll tell her 'no' when she's wrong and pull her up when she's depressed." Ming poked his arm. "Like us!" She put her arm through his as they walked toward his car. "I think Tom is the type who'll agree with everything she says and drown in her darkness when she's sad. Annie's a smart girl. She'll figure it out."

Tom's car passed the two of them, and Annie was upset to see Emir and Ming walking so close together. She was uncharacteristically silent during brunch.

Father Sullivan wasn't surprised that Bishop Milano called that afternoon. "What's going on down there, John? My phone's been ringing off the hook."

The priest wiped his forehead. "Well, Your Excellency, I believe that one of my young parishioners is experiencing a demonic possession, and that's what responsible for the unrest. I wish to perform an exorcism."

"Have you talked to her parents?"

"Her father's deceased, and I haven't spoken to her mother since the child began to show these dramatic behavioral changes."

The bishop sighed. "You know that you'll need to have a physician rule out mental illness as the underlying cause of her symptoms, and you'll need the mother's consent before you can conduct an exorcism."

"Yes, Your Excellency."

"Okay, John. Meanwhile, I think you need to let the situation cool off. I've asked Father Donovan from Boca Raton to say your Sunday Mass for the next few weeks."

"Thank you, Your Excellency."

"Go with God, my son."

Chapter 22

Father Sullivan called Colleen on Monday to ask if they could meet to discuss the escalating situation. She consented to stop by the rectory later in the afternoon. He advised her not to mention the impending visit to Annie, and she agreed that her daughter didn't have to know since it would only upset her.

Colleen arrived on time, and when the housekeeper showed her into Father Sullivan's study, she was surprised to find that she was nervous. They had been friends for almost twenty years, and she had never experienced this feeling. Something was up.

The priest downed a shot of bourbon and walked into the room to greet his estranged friend. "Colleen, thank you for coming in these troubled times."

She backed away as he tried to hug her, so he extended his hand, which she ignored. "John, one of my daughter's friends was shot. Another one was attacked, and my house was set on fire because of your words. I don't think this is a friendly visit."

He shook his head slightly. "I asked you to come today because I'm genuinely worried about Annie."

Colleen's features softened a little. "I know, John. I'm worried myself. She's had a lot to cope with during a short period of time. She hasn't been the same since Craig died."

He gave her a tissue and invited her to sit down across from him. "Craig was a good man and a good friend of mine. He was like a brother to me. I miss him too." He shifted in his seat as he crossed his legs. "Has Annie seen a doctor?"

Colleen wiped a tear from her cheek. "Since the shark attack, she's started seeing Dr. Lamberti again. I think it's helping, but she's still not right. I'm afraid she may be mentally ill. But, I have to trust Dr. Lamberti's opinion, and she's not diagnosing Annie with an illness. Thank God, Annie's making good friends."

He smiled ruefully. "I've met her friends."

Colleen smiled for the first time. "They aren't making things easy for you. But, the good news is that Annie's recovering in spite of it all, and she's agreed to go back to public school in September."

Father Sullivan leaned forward in his chair. "She may be recovering, but you know she's not the same girl." He paused for a moment. "How's her physical health?"

Colleen sighed. "She doesn't sleep well. We had tests done last week. The EEG was slightly abnormal, but that's apparently fairly common in people who've survived a near-death experience. It seems to permanently change the brain." Colleen wiped her cheek again. "Annie will tell you it's because she's now more in touch with the Universe." Tears welled up in her eyes. "The neurologists say it's nothing to worry about. They say she's fine."

Father Sullivan sat back as he uncrossed his legs. "I don't think she's fine."

Colleen clenched her fist as her pulse began to race. She spoke in a raspy voice. "What are you talking about?"

Their eyes locked for what seemed like an eternity before he continued his thought. "I think she's being unnaturally influenced."

Colleen's heart was about to burst through her chest. She leaned towards him, her face a mask of anguish, and whispered, "What are you saying?"

His composure began to crumble as he took her hand. "Colleen... "

She shook off his hand and jumped up, looming over him. "Just say it!" She almost spat out the words.

He took a deep breath and looked up at her with pain in his eyes. "I think something happened out there in the water. Something bad."

She slapped him, and he grabbed her wrist and held on until she calmed down. "Colleen, I think the devil entered her soul when she stopped breathing."

"No... not my baby!"

The priest stood up. "Now he's using her to disrupt the Church."

Colleen collapsed on the tile floor, sobbing uncontrollably. Finally, she recovered enough to force out a few words. "What can we do?"

He knelt down beside her and took both of her hands. "I can perform an exorcism."

She shuttered as she realized that this was the idea she'd been fighting for weeks. "Do they really work?"

He sat back on his heels. "Sometimes, other times it can take years of sessions."

Colleen wasn't persuaded. "Will she be hurt?"

"Probably not, but the devil is very strong and cares nothing about hurting her body." There was a moment of silence. "Do you want me to do it?"

Colleen put her head in her hands. "I have to pray about it. I'll let you know what I decide."

Annie and Tom wanted to spend his last day together, so she suggested a visit to the Everglades National Park. Her father had started taking her there when she was five, and it was one of her favorite places. The north entrance to the park, which is 30 miles due west of Miami, would be an easy drive from Emir's house.

It was a scorching hot day, so the two decided not to rent bicycles. Instead, Tom purchased a bird-watching booklet at the gift shop, and they bought tickets for the two-hour narrated tram tour. This area of the park has a 15-mile paved road that loops among the sawgrass marsh, and Annie and her father had enjoyed cycling the route in the cool winter weather.

The park rancher was a terrific guide and pointed out the birds, deer, pythons and gators as Annie and Tom sat safely in the covered tram. Halfway through the tour, the vehicle stopped at a 65-foot observation tower that provided a panoramic view of the park. Tom was amazed that the sunlight seemed softer here, and the clouds looked different than they did over a city.

He understood why Annie loved the place, but he wished it was cooler. His constant complaints about the heat were getting on Annie's nerves, and she was glad when the tour was over. She knew it took time to adapt to the temperature and humidity, but she didn't want to hear about it. He kept it up, even after they were back in the air-conditioned car, and she finally had enough and told him to shut up. He tried to change the subject, but Annie was silent for the rest of the drive home.

When they pulled into Emir's driveway, he started making excuses for his comments. But, Annie didn't want to listen and jumped out of the car without saying goodbye. A discouraged Tom shook his head, gunned the engine and took off.

A smiling Emir greeted Annie at the door, but she blew past him and slammed the door to her bedroom. Too late, she saw Ming sitting on her bed, painting her toenails blue.

Ming looked up. "What's wrong with you?"

Annie blurted out the words. "All Tom does is complain!"

"You guys have a fight?"

Annie stomped her foot in frustration. "He kept complaining about the heat. Like a whining little kid. I can't stand it!"

Ming grinned. "Sounds to me like you're over-reacting. Maybe you're trying to pick a fight, so it's easier to see him leave."

Annie groaned. "Sounds like you've been through this before."

Chapter Twenty-Two

Ming snorted. "Many times."

Annie sat on her bed and started picking at her face. After a few minutes, she calmed down and made her decision. "You're right. I should apologize."

They talked for an hour on the phone, and Tom promised to text her at least once a day after he got back to Ohio. Annie replayed her favorite memories of him until she could no longer keep her eyes open. Emotionally exhausted, she fell into a deep sleep.

Pumpkin.

Her father was dressed all in white. *Daddy?*

There's danger ahead.

What kind of danger?

Your mother.

Mom's going to hurt me?

Be careful.

Daddy, what's going to happen?

Stay with friends.

Daddy!

Don't be alone, pumpkin.

Chapter 23

The Sunday protest in the church quickly went viral. The national networks picked up the local feed, which was followed by airings on BBC, CNN and Al Jazeera. By Tuesday afternoon, the YouTube upload had more than one million viewings.

Kids around the world divided themselves into pro-Annie and anti-Annie camps. Those in favor of the movement wore the approved T-shirt, and the opposition had its own shirts printed that depicted Annie as the devil and the priest as the angel.

Fights broke out, which brought even more attention to the movement. Three teens were arrested in London for disturbing the peace, and a riot erupted in Rome when the police cracked down on the kids wearing the devil-priest shirts.

The Turkish response was overwhelmingly positive since one of their own had become an overnight role model for Muslim boys everywhere. The country was bursting with pride to have a globally recognized hero with Turkish roots.

Likewise, Chinese teenagers adopted Ming as their favorite public figure, and spiky wigs were flying off the shelves. The cosmetic saleswomen quickly learned how to create Ming's Cleopatra eyes for their customers. Pastel eyeshadow replaced the popular browns and grays, and heavy black eyeliner was in high demand. Ming was suddenly a fashion queen for Chinese girls and received hundreds of emailed requests for photo shoots.

Entrepreneurs in India printed T-shirts of Annie with a third eye in the middle of her forehead. This depiction of her psychic abilities was very popular, and the shirts sold so well that Emir decided to sell similar ones on their own website. Ming suggested that they start marketing sunglasses with a third lens that stuck up and covered the imaginary eye in the center of the forehead, and Emir agreed to contact possible manufacturers. Telepathy was finally getting some positive recognition. After all, the movement was more about sending peace messages and less about the kids' personalities and appearance.

Another sign that the message was getting through was the hundreds of peace songs appearing on the Internet. Although most of them were amateurish productions by fledgling songwriters, some professionals were joining in and making the songs available for free. The most popular websites crashed two or three times a day because of the volume of requested downloads. It seemed that the songs were available in every language on the planet. The local radio stations began playing the better ones, and people were humming the tunes as they went about their day. Many of the songs appealed to music lovers of all ages, and this was the first dramatic sign that the movement was enjoying a positive acceptance by the older generation.

The most polarizing response to Sunday's activities occurred in Catholics. Some were horrified that the kids would stage a protest during Mass, but other equally religious people blamed the priest for aggravating the situation and became ardent supporters. Although the conservative news station reported the situation as a fight between good (the priest) and evil (the kids), most of the other news channels produced more unbiased telecasts.

Father Sullivan would never admit it, but there was a part of him that resented the attention the kids were getting. He had ministered to his parishioners for more than 20 years, living a lonely life in obscurity trying to do God's work. Now, three teenagers say they are responding to a message from the Other Side to bring peace to the world, and they are an instant sensation. Although he sincerely believed the devil was involved, their popularity irked him.

Since he didn't know if Colleen would consent to the exorcism, he had to come up with a backup plan to stop the trio from causing further damage to the Church and his own reputation. He needed more information about them. The priest knew that he would never get past the guards in Emir's subdivision, so he had to figure out another way to find out what they were up to.

As he paced up and down in his study, he considered his options. Another television interview would be pointless unless he had something new to say, and since the bishop was replacing him at Sunday Mass, he no longer had the opportunity to address the topic during his sermons. He was at a loss for what to do next.

Discouraged, he sat in front of his computer pondering his dilemma. Finally, while he was reading emails from his supporters, an idea hit him. It intrigued him, but he immediately rejected it because it was illegal. He went back to scanning his mail, but the idea wouldn't leave him alone. No matter what he did, he couldn't shake the feeling that this was what he had to do. After a sleepless night, he decided to call one of his supportive parishioners who had disclosed some criminal activity during confession.

His hands were shaking so badly that he had to lay the phone on the table and turn on the speaker. "Hi, Bob. It's Father Sullivan. I've got a job for you if you're interested, and I'll pay you well for your discretion."

Chapter 24

Bob Greene was a church-going, God-fearing, middle-aged man with one vice. He enjoyed hacking into computer systems, and he was very good at it. He didn't do it to plant viruses or steal credit card information. He simply enjoyed the challenge and liked to snoop, and now he was Father Sullivan's go-to guy.

The job wasn't a difficult one. Father Sullivan asked him to break into Annie's, Emir's and Ming's computers and look around for information that might be used against them. None of the kids used password protection, so he completed his task within a couple of hours.

Bob accessed their website and traced the IP address for the blog posts back to Emir's computer where emails led him to the girls' systems. It was a piece of cake that yielded a gold mine of potentially useful information. He reported his findings to the priest and sat back to watch the fireworks.

Father Sullivan was now armed and ready to do battle. He wanted to go public in a big way, so he called his friends at his favorite news station, and they invited him to fly up to New York for a Thursday night interview. He immediately accepted and began to prepare his talking points.

The priest's primary goal was to dethrone the kids and damage their credibility. Fortunately for him, Bob had discovered a daily online journal in Emir's computer that provided plenty of ammunition. The hard part was deciding what to use without tipping his hand. He didn't want them to suspect that anyone had breached their Internet security because he might decide to have Bob continually monitor their activities. However, that would be an expensive proposition, and he'd have to take some time to consider it.

On Thursday night, Annie and Emir took a seat in front of Emir's television waiting to hear what new insults Father Sullivan would hurl at them. Ming walked in and set a bowl of popcorn on the coffee table, so they would have something to throw at the screen during his attack.

Once the introductions were over, the interviewer quickly got down to business. "Father Sullivan, why don't you tell the viewers why you're here tonight."

The priest coughed, took a sip of water and began to speak. "Thank you, Maria. I'm here to talk about the peace movement that started in Fort Lauderdale and has gained the attention of the world within a very short time."

Maria nodded. "Yes, it's remarkable the way it's spreading like wildfire."

He hesitated for a moment. "I believe people are putting these teenagers on a pedestal without knowing what they're really like."

Maria frowned. "Oh, what do you mean?"

He ran his hand through his hair. "I recently received some confidential information that will change people's opinion about them."

Maria leaned toward him. "You have millions of viewers waiting to hear what you have to say."

That was music to the priest's ears. "I have reason to believe that neither Annie nor Emir is mentally stable. They are deceiving people and can't be trusted."

"What do you mean?"

"Someone close to Annie believes that she may be mentally ill."

"That's a very harsh statement, Father. Who is this person?"

The priest was angry that his statement was being questioned. "Her mother!" He instantly regretted his words, but it was too late.

Maria was taken aback. "Are you telling me that Annie McDoogan's mother personally told you that she thinks her daughter may be mentally ill?"

He shrugged and looked down at the floor. "Yes."

"Why would she tell you such a thing?"

He might as well get it all out in the open. "We were discussing the possibility of an exorcism."

"What?"

He wiped the sweat from his forehead. "It's no secret that I think Annie may be possessed. I'm one of the few approved exorcists in Florida, and I was asking her mother for permission to conduct the ritual."

"This is news. What was the mother's response?"

"She's considering it."

Maria glanced down at her notes. "You also mentioned Emir in your opening remarks. What have you found out about him?"

Father Sullivan wiped his palms on his trousers and folded his hands in front of him. "This young man is not what he seems. He's a liar, and he's mentally unstable."

Maria almost spat out the water she had just sipped. "You're saying this teen idol is a liar? That's hard to believe."

The priest almost stood up. How dare she question his honesty! Who does she think she is? He took a few moments to calm down before answering. "*My* honesty is unquestionable. I have it from a reliable source that Emir didn't accidentally overdose while he was studying for an exam. He deliberately tried to commit suicide and lied to cover it up!"

Chapter 25

"Liar!" Annie jumped up from her seat waving her fist at the TV. She turned to look at Emir. "Tell me he's lying, Emir. Tell me!"

Ming was also on her feet shouting at everyone. "Who the hell does he think he is?"

Annie grabbed Emir's arm. "Come on, Emir, say something!"

Emir slumped over, burying his head in his hands. Without thinking, Ming rushed to his side, throwing her arms around his shoulders while she held him close. Annie collapsed at his feet, reaching up to touch his hands. His pain washed over and through them, burning its way through their souls.

Annie finally broke the silence as she gently pulled his hands away from his face and whispered in a soft voice. "Tell us."

Emir's eyes were dark pools of sadness as he looked at Annie's anguished expression. "It's true. I didn't accidentally overdose. I was trying to kill myself."

Ming rubbed his shoulder. "Why? Why would you do that?"

He shook his head slightly. "At the time, it seemed like the best way out."

Annie unconsciously dug her fingernails into his knees. "What are you talking about?"

Emir sighed as he removed Annie's hands. "I didn't want to disappoint my parents. They had mapped out my college-prep courses and my career, and I knew I was going to fail my AP Biology exam." He rubbed his forehead. "There is so much pressure. Pressure to be good in school. Pressure to be a good Muslim. Pressure to be a doctor. On that particular night, it was just too much."

Ming turned his head toward hers. "How do you feel now?"

He smiled. "Better. The funny thing is that the psychic I talked to in Cassadaga knew I had attempted suicide. When I asked him if my parents would be happy if I decided to spend my life healing people, he said no. So, it looks like no matter what I do, I'm bound to disappoint them. In a weird way, that makes things easier."

Annie took his hand. "How do you think Father Sullivan found out?"

Emir shrugged. "Who knows? I was around a lot of people that night and was probably rambling. He could have heard it from a paramedic, nurse or another patient that was in the emergency room at the same time as me. I'll probably never know."

Annie smiled for the first time. "You know this means that your parents will want to have a nice long chat with you tonight."

He groaned. "Speaking of parents, I wonder where they are."

Annie frowned. "They're watching the show with my mom in the study. They're probably in shock and trying to decide what psychiatrist to send you to."

Emir chuckled. "I've heard good things about Dr. Lamberti."

Annie's eyes twinkled. "She's great, and she's already heard a lot about you."

Emir pushed her away. "Can't wait. Now get off the floor." He held his hand out to help her up. "Ming, you can get off me too."

Ming was happy to see that he was himself again. "Okay, okay. But, I'd like to stay."

He laughed. "Scram!" His smile disappeared as he turned his attention back to Annie. "Your turn."

Annie's heart started racing. "What do you mean?"

Emir folded his arms across his chest. "You fight a shark instead of running away. You tried to run onto a stage to get Ming when you could've been shot, and you try your best to go into a room that's on fire." He stood up and leaned over her chair. "I asked you this before, and I didn't get an answer. Answer me now! Are you trying to kill yourself?"

Ming gasped, and Annie's hands started to shake. "Not... not... not intentionally." She couldn't stop stuttering. "I... I... I... don't know. I... I... I... miss daddy."

Emir leaned in closer and peered into her watery eyes. "I can't lose you. Your cause has become my cause and gives meaning to my life." He backed off and pointed his finger at her. "Do you understand? You have to stop this reckless behavior!"

Ming walked over to Annie and sat on the arm of her chair. She put her arm around her friend. "He's right, Annie. You've changed both of us in a way that's hard to explain." Ming gave her a quick hug. "We need you. We're better people because of you. Our near-death experiences made us want to make our lives matter, but we didn't know how to do it until we met you."

Annie smiled. "So you don't think I'm possessed?"

Ming shook her. "Girl, you may be crazy, but you're an angel. A good angel."

Emir interrupted her. He didn't want anyone calling Annie crazy, not even Ming. "Speaking of crazy, what's up with your mother? You haven't said a word about her talking to Father Sullivan about you. What gives? I'd be furious if I were you. Heck, I *am* furious. She had no right to do that."

Annie let out a loud sigh and stretched in the chair. "You don't understand. Father John was such a good friend of daddy's that talking to him helps her. I think she sort of feels like she's talking to dad again." She shrugged. "So, what can I say? We miss daddy in our own ways and cope with our loss in different ways. I'm not saying it's healthy. I'm just saying that's the way it is."

Emir nodded, and Ming squeezed her shoulder. "We get it, girlfriend. Now it's my turn. I wasn't outed on the show like the two of you were, but I've got my own secret."

They looked at her expectantly. "While you two are dreaming up ways to off yourselves, I've actually killed someone."

Emir's and Annie's mouths dropped open. "What?"

Ming stared at the floor. "Oh, I didn't shoot anybody or throw a knife in their heart, but I might as well have." She fiddled with her earrings for a minute. "I was responsible for the crash that killed my date. He didn't swerve to avoid a dog. He lost control when I started nibbling on his ear. If I had stayed in my seat, he'd be alive. I lied to the police, and it's my fault that he's dead. I'll have that on my conscience for the rest of my life." She wiped a tear from her eye. "I killed him."

Emir's father reached over and turned off the intercom. As shocked as they were by the broadcast, the pain in their children's voices broke their hearts. Without thinking about it, Colleen, Daphne and Mehmet joined hands and prayed for those wounded kids bonding together in the next room.

When they finished, Daphne turned toward Colleen. "I don't mean to intrude in your business, but Mehmet and I have grown very fond of Annie, and we think you're making a big mistake."

Mehmet nodded his agreement. "Yes. Over the years, Daphne and I have both had patients who died on the operating table. I'm telling you that there was no pulse, but we continued to perform CPR, and a few of those patients revived. Almost all of them had stories of floating over their bodies and moving toward the light."

Daphne was becoming more animated. "Most of them talked about feeling the presence of other souls, but Annie is the one receiving the most publicity because she wants to put that knowledge to practical use. You have a remarkable child, Colleen, whether you realize it or not."

Colleen resented the inference that they knew her daughter better than she did, and she excused herself and went to her bedroom when her cell started ringing. She heard from every one of her family members and Craig's. No one wanted to listen to her concerns. The overwhelming response was that she was crazy and that Annie was the best daughter that she could possibly have.

How could she make them understand the changes in Annie's personality? They saw her on TV and thought she was becoming a superstar. They didn't see that she was undermining the Church and mocking people's belief in the power of prayer. The fighting in the streets proved that Annie was causing violence, not bringing peace. Father John was right, and God was on their side.

She'd call Dr. Lamberti next week and clear it with her. She knew the doctor would try and talk her out of it, but unless she could say that Annie was mentally ill, the priest had the right to perform the exorcism. Now that her mind was made up, Colleen relaxed and slept like a baby.

Emir's parents went to bed without talking to him.

Chapter 26

Annie was up early the next morning and surprised everyone at the breakfast table by wearing shorts for the first time in Emir's home. No one mentioned it, and Annie seemed oblivious to the ugly scar on her thigh. However, when Ming appeared in a pool cover-up without a wig or makeup, Emir couldn't keep silent.

"Look at you! There's a real girl underneath all the extra hair and goop."

Ming wasn't sure that was much of a compliment but decided to smile sweetly at him anyway as she grabbed an apple off the table. "Thanks. I'm having trouble writing the lyrics for one of my new songs, so I thought that I'd relax in your pool while you and Annie defend yourselves on our website."

Annie's jaw dropped. She didn't think Ming even owned a bathing suit. "You know how to swim?"

"I can dog paddle or float if I have to. Emir, do you have a raft I can use?"

"It's in the cabana. Help yourself."

"Cool. You two have fun."

It turned out to be a double-whammy day for the peace movement. When Emir and Annie logged into their computers, they were astounded to see that they had more than 3,000 emails waiting for them. It didn't take long for them to realize that the magazine interview had hit the newsstands that morning. Maddie's article, combined with reaction to Father Sullivan's television interview, was generating a firestorm of angry protests. Since many of the emails were hours old, Emir and Ming decided to focus on the live news feeds to see if tempers had cooled off. What they saw made them sick.

Violent confrontations were erupting everywhere. Buddhist and Muslim extremists wanted retribution for Ming's and Emir's public rejection of fundamental religious principles. The fact that they publicly rebuked reincarnation and the Islamic belief in the storage of souls infuriated many believers. They felt that the kids were using their international platform to ridicule their religion and turn people away from the righteous path. The turmoil increased as word spread, and copies of the magazine article made its way into the hands of the angry fundamentalists. They wanted revenge.

The Islamic response was the most extreme. Mannequins dressed to look like Emir were burnt and stoned throughout the Middle East. Kids painted his face on their soccer balls and screamed as they kicked him. One particularly troubling video showed a straw-filled Emir hung from the ceiling like a piñata, spinning in circles as teenage boys hit him with a bat, cheering as his insides spilled out onto the floor.

The most tragic event occurred in Ankara, Turkey, when teenage girls linked arms to resist the oncoming wave of protesting boys. Emotions ran high as the boys forced their way through the lines, trampling three young girls who had tripped and found themselves pinned to the ground under the feet of their rampaging classmates. Their screams went unheard over the roar of the crowd, and their suffering bodies lay unseen in the street until the police broke up the riot. Ambulances rushed to the scene, but it was too late. The girls were dead, and the former golden boy was now a pariah.

The Buddhist reaction also resulted in unforeseen tragedies. Television cameras captured shots of fanatics marching in the streets and burning wigs. One boy reached into a fire to save a picture of Ming, but the bonfire collapsed around him, and he burned to death. Another died when shots that were fired into the air ricocheted off a building and struck him in his chest. The few monks who consented to interviews tried to calm the fervor. They emphasized that people can choose the parts of Buddhism that work for them. They might not be considered Buddhists if they don't believe in reincarnation, but they could certainly continue to follow their individual path to enlightenment. One girl's ideas weren't going to change a religion that had existed for more than 2,000 years. They pleaded with people to meditate and remain calm.

Fights over Father Sullivan's remarks were as violent as the religious protests. Police were called in to break up conflicts in London, Paris, Barcelona, Mexico City, Rio, Toronto, Los Angeles, Chicago, Houston and Atlanta. Cars were overturned and burned. Teens threw bricks through store windows and carried off what they wanted. Broken noses caused blood to flow on both sides. Annie's supporters around the world fought hard to defend her reputation, but Annie's most personally painful tragedy occurred in Fort Lauderdale.

Word had gone out that Annie's supporters were going to meet under the trees outside the Science Museum to plan their strategy for counteracting the charges against her. There was plenty of shade, and nearby vendors had cold drinks for sale. Everyone was relaxed, and the crowd had a festive air as the kids mingled and high-fived each other.

Exactly at noon, a caravan of cars rolled up. One by one, the drivers let out their occupants and drove away. As the new arrivals increased in number, they began to move toward Annie's supporters. Slowly and deliberately, they inched closer. Most were boys who were too young to shave but old enough to fight. Kids who had too much time on their hands on a hot summer day. Kids itching for some action.

The only sound was the slamming of car doors. No birds. No squirrels. Just ominous silence.

"Hey, loser! Go home!"

The fuse was lit, and the dynamite exploded. Fists were flying, and curses split the air. The two sides were evenly matched, and no obvious winner was emerging.

The sound of police sirens sent many of the kids running toward Las Olas Boulevard. Others were too caught up in the adrenaline of the fight to leave. The police moved in and tried to separate the fighting pairs. When that failed, they fired off tear gas at the crowd. But, the breeze was too strong, and the gas disappeared too quickly to be effective. In desperation, the cops reached for their Tasers.

No one could accuse the police of discrimination that day. Boys, girls, black, brown, white and yellow were all targets. No one was spared. The officers hit whomever they could reach. One thin boy stopped fighting and begged the officer to leave him alone. But, the cop was also caught up in the mob mentality, and his Taser fired before he even realized it. The boy collapsed on the ground, shaking uncontrollably until his heart stopped beating, and all movements ceased.

A gifted artist died that day, for he was the one who had drawn the picture of the angelic warrior Annie on the church wall so many weeks ago. He had become a good friend of Annie's, and his death sent her into a downward spiral.

Televangelists wasted no time grabbing the spotlight and condemning Annie for all the deaths. Charges of satanic possession and mental illness took over the airwaves. The preachers shouted their accusations at the unseen Annie, and Father Sullivan breathed a sigh of relief that they were supporting him in his efforts to stop the kids. He regretted the deaths but considered them collateral damage in his war against evil.

Chapter 27

Ming and Emir decided they needed to try to pull Annie out of her nosedive. They knew she was drowning in guilt over the recent deaths and thought a change of scenery would do them all some good. Annie wasn't the only one who felt guilty. Ming and Emir shared that burden with her.

No rain was in the forecast, so Emir called one of his friends and asked to borrow his boat for a few hours. His friend agreed, so Ming pulled Annie out of bed and persuaded her to go with them. Colleen packed a picnic lunch for them with plenty of bottled water, and off they went. Ming even let Annie sit in the front seat. Emir put the top down, and their spirits improved as they got closer to the marina.

Annie was used to boats since her father would take her out on patrol with him sometimes when his commander was off-duty. She loved the spray of water on her face and the lurch in her stomach when a boat cut through the waves.

Ming had never been on a boat and looked forward to the experience. She'd always felt that she was missing out on a lot of fun by never going to the ocean. Maybe they could all take sailing lessons together. It seemed like such a romantic thing to do, sailing in the moonlight without a care in the world. Maybe knowing how to sail would get her a movie role some day.

First, she'd have to take swimming lessons. She had stretched the truth a little when she told Annie she could float and dog paddle. She could keep her head above water but didn't know how to move forward. She guessed that she could figure it out if she ever had to.

Emir parked the car, unloaded the cooler and spotted his friend's boat tied to the dock. They were all excited about going out on the water and failed to notice the gray pickup driving slowly by the marina. The sun was shining, and the winds were calm. Nothing was going to ruin this day. Not even the fact that there were no life preservers or jackets on board.

Emir knew that he shouldn't go out without them but decided to risk it just this once. Nobody he knew had ever actually needed them, so the chances were slim that anything would happen to the three of them. He asked the girls what they wanted to do, and they agreed with his decision. So, off they went.

Emir expertly motored through Port Everglades and out to the open ocean. Annie kept a sharp eye out for fins in the water. She had to admit that being on the water was causing her to experience some flashbacks of the shark attack. Emir noticed that she was looking a little green and understood the reason for it. He asked her to captain the boat in order to get her mind off of sharks. She gladly took over the wheel and rewarded him with a grateful smile and a bottle of water.

They decided to go as far north as Lighthouse Point and then come back south on the Intracoastal Waterway. Ming would get a kick out of seeing some of the waterfront mansions on the canal. Maybe they'd see a manatee or two if they were lucky. Annie cut the engine off the Fort Lauderdale beach, and Emir dropped the anchor, being careful not to hit the coral reef, so they could eat without worrying about the boat drifting into swimmers. Emir took the cooler to the back of the boat, and they joined Ming on the sunny, padded seats.

It was noon, and they were almost alone on the water. The scuba operators had finished their morning dives and wouldn't be back out until 1:30, and it was too calm for sailing or windsurfing. There were a few people on the sand, but there were no lifeguards on this part of the beach. The only boat Emir could see was coming up fast from the south. Too fast. The hairs on the back of his neck bristled.

"Annie, take the wheel."

She could tell from his voice that something was wrong and ran to the front. Emir started yanking up the 40 feet of anchor chain. "When I tell you to go, head for Lighthouse Point. Ming, go up by Annie and get ready to call 911. Annie, give her our coordinates when she calls."

They were tense and ready. Annie was worried about Ming. "Ming, if you have to jump, head toward the beach. We're close to shore and the tide's coming in. You can float to shore."

Ming confessed in a small, pitiful voice. "I don't know how to float."

Annie was surprised. "But you said—"

Emir interrupted. "I'll take care of her. We'll make it." He finally got the anchor up. "Go, go, go!"

Ming called 911 to report a possible pursuit while Annie pushed the boat as fast as it would go. But, the other boat was faster. Emir found a pair of binoculars and grunted. "Same guys who attacked me at the church."

"Emir, get the wheel. I'll stay with Ming. I'm going to call my dad's coast guard unit. They're based at the Point, and I know that they'll help if they can. Anyway, I'm afraid I'll get stuck on the sandbar at the mouth of the inlet if we get that far. You're better at this than I am."

Annie was on the phone for less than a minute. "Guard's on its way! They set off the sirens while I was still on the phone."

Ming called 911 and gave them the update. "The police dispatcher said the patrol boat has already left the port. She'll tell them the guys are wanted men."

Emir wiped the spray off his face. "Okay, the police are coming from the south, and the coast guard is coming from the north. We'll be sandwiched between them, and the other boat won't get away no matter what happens. We've got them."

Ming was trembling. "Or they get us first."

Annie put her arm around her and squeezed. "We'll be okay." *I hope.*

Emir glanced back at the other boat that was gaining fast. "Hang on. They're going to ram us!"

The words were barely out of his mouth when the boat lurched forward and threw Ming overboard. She screamed as she dropped into the water. Annie jumped in right after her. "We're okay. Go!" She flashed a thumbs-up to Emir, in case he didn't hear her.

She quickly turned to the flailing Ming whose eyes were wide with fright. "Listen to me. We have to dive to avoid getting hit by the boats. Keep your eyes open and hold my hand. Take a deep breath. Now!"

Emir panicked when he saw them submerge. For a moment, every instinct in his body told him to dive in and save them. Every nerve in his body was firing, and his brain was spinning as he tried to grasp what was happening and weigh the danger. After a minute, he understood Annie's plan and knew he had to lead the other boat away before the girls were hurt.

Ming was numb with shock, and her responses were on autopilot. She gulped some air and allowed Annie to lead her down and toward the beach. She mimicked Annie's kicks, and they made good progress.

Emir's boat didn't appear to be damaged, so he gunned the engine and headed north. As he did, he saw the U.S. flag and knew the Coast Guard had arrived. He made a U-turn and followed them back to the scene.

The attack boat also saw the flag and turned and headed south. When they saw the blue lights of the police boat, they spun their boat toward land. They flew over the submerged Annie and Ming and ran the boat up on the beach. The police boat was closing fast.

After two minutes, Ming couldn't hold her breath any longer, and they had to come up for air. The first thing Annie heard as she broke the surface was the blare of a horn and an urgent booming voice.

"Cut your engines! Cut your engines! Swimmers starboard! Swimmers starboard!" The amplified voice was coming from the Coast Guard cutter in front of her. Who were they talking to?

Annie looked south and saw the police boat headed straight for them! Without thinking, she grabbed Ming's hand and pulled her down under the water. Ming wasn't prepared and struggled to get back to the surface for air. Annie fought to keep her down. She saw the boat zoom by overhead and started to pull Ming toward the surface.

She wasn't coming up! Ming's foot lodged under a ledge, and she couldn't break free. Her leg scraped against the sharp coral. Blood!

Annie's nightmares returned. *Oh, God. Oh, God. Oh, God. Please, no sharks. God, please, no sharks.*

Panic overwhelmed Ming. *I can't breathe. I need air! Annie!*

Emir was on the deck watching the surface for any sign of his friends. Coast Guard divers were already in the water and told him to stay out. Pacing, pacing, pacing. Back and forth, looking for a sign. Pulling his hair. Watching the water. *Blood! What happened? Why aren't they coming up? It's been too long. Annie!*

Annie freed a limp Ming and frantically hauled her to the surface. The divers took over and quickly hoisted Ming up and onto the deck. A crew member threw her a life preserver, and Annie was temporarily left alone in the water, her eyes darting back and forth, searching for deadly black fins. Her breathing was fast and shallow. Emir saw what was happening and dived in. He couldn't stand it. He had to let her know that everything was okay. She clung to him and wouldn't let go as he whispered assurances in her ear and stroked her hair. She closed her eyes and let the warmth of his body soothe her.

A paramedic immediately started CPR and turned Ming on her side when she began spitting up salt water. The crew cheered, and Annie and Emir looked up and saw a dazed Ming sitting up. They broke their embrace and made their way to the boat's ladder. There were more cheers as the crew recognized their familiar red-haired visitor. A joyful Annie knew most of them, and her smile lit up the faces around her.

"Did they catch the men?"

"Don't know. The police are chasing them on foot."

Chapter 28

Annie, Ming and Emir finished their lunch on land after returning the boat to its berth. There was some cosmetic damage that Emir would have to pay to have fixed. Other than that, they were in pretty good shape, all things considered.

Ming forgave Annie for drowning her, and Annie felt bad about that until Emir pointed out that the police boat would have ripped Ming's head off if Annie hadn't dunked her. That cheered everybody up, and they attacked their sandwiches with gusto.

Halfway through her tuna fish sub, Ming paused for a minute. "I guess that takes care of my water warning."

"Huh?" Neither Annie nor Emir knew what she was talking about.

"The psychic. She told me to watch out for water."

Annie snapped her fingers. "Mine told me to beware of a gray truck. The guys in the boat own the truck, so maybe we're off the hook now for two of the warnings."

Emir shook his head. "The police didn't catch them. They're still out there and probably hate us more than ever now."

Annie hit the table. "Hate us more? How can they possibly hate us any more?"

Emir stared at her. "They haven't tried to kill us yet."

Annie had a puzzled look. "How'd they find us?"

Emir thought for a minute. "They must have put a tracking bug on my car when I was at the mosque one Friday night."

Ming didn't feel like talking about gloom and doom. "Can we change the conversation? Annie, you were mighty chummy with the rescue crew. What'd you talk about?"

Annie smiled. "They were my dad's friends, and I know a lot of them. They've been following the news about us."

Ming looked up from her plate. "Do they support us?"

"Of course! They said that I was just like my dad." Her face fell as she remembered something else. "They also knew about Father Sullivan's remarks about mom."

Annie sighed. "One of them said it was common for victim's survivors to become hyper-religious. He told me to get her into professional counseling with someone other than Father Sullivan." She grabbed a fry before continuing. "They all know Father John and think he's a victim's survivor the same way mom is. He was dad's best friend for a lot of years."

Emir frowned. "So, the two of them are feeding each other's pain, and nobody is recovering?"

Annie nodded. "That about sums it up. After dad died, they reached out to her, but she just withdrew."

Ming finished off the rest of the fries. "How do you tell your mother that she needs a psychiatrist?"

Colleen was worried. Annie told her to go see Dr. Lamberti, and she was turning the Polats against her. This wasn't her Annie. It must be the work of Satan, and it was time for her to act. Her first call was to Dr. Lamberti, who confirmed that Annie had not been diagnosed with a mental illness, but she begged Colleen not to go through with an exorcism. She told her that Annie was too emotionally fragile to be subjected to any more stress. Colleen hung up on her and called Father Sullivan and told him to get ready. Then she went to wake up her daughter.

"Rise and shine, Annie. I need your help today."

She groaned and snuggled deeper under her comforter. "Noooo."

"Come on. Get up. I think it's time we bought Emir and his parents a thank-you gift."

That caught Annie's attention. They deserved a present even if it meant she had to take a shower and get dressed. She rolled over to face her mother, but Colleen wouldn't look her in the eye. What was going on? "Give me 45 minutes."

After she showered, Annie went in search of Emir. She found him in the kitchen and pushed him into the utility room. His back was against the washing machine as she started whispering quickly. "Mom said she's taking me shopping, but she's up to something, and I don't think it's good. My phone's GPS is on. Can you track me?"

Emir frowned. "Yes... "

Annie relaxed a little. "Okay. I'm going to text you once an hour. If you don't hear from me, come and get me. No matter what."

Colleen's driving was fast and erratic. "Slow down, Mom!"

Colleen wiped her damp palms on her slacks and tried to focus on the traffic. She slowed down a bit. "Sorry, honey."

Annie turned to look at her mother. "Where are we going?"

Colleen kept her eyes on the road as she clenched the steering wheel. "Father John wants to talk to you. I think that he wants to apologize."

Annie turned away and rested her head against the window. "I don't want to talk to him."

The sun warmed her cheek, and she closed her eyes. All she wanted was to sleep. This whole thing had been a mistake. People were dead, and it was her fault. Maybe she had just imagined seeing her father. It seemed like a bad dream now. She just wanted to sleep. Let Emir handle it.

Annie woke when the car jerked to a stop at the rectory. "All right, let's get this over with."

She lethargically followed Colleen into the rectory, but her senses jolted awake when she saw the priest. He didn't look apologetic. He looked smug.

He directed Annie to sit in the wooden armchair next to his desk. Once she was seated, Colleen came and stood behind her. Annie sensed the rising tension in the room. *This is weird.*

Father Sullivan reached over and took both of Annie's hands. His eyes narrowed, and his breath smelled sour as he leaned into her face. "You've caused the death of innocent people, and this must stop today."

Annie's eyes widened as Colleen gripped her shoulders. *Oh hell, he's going through with the exorcism.* She struggled as their holds tightened. Father Sullivan leaned even closer. "I'm going to drive the devil out of you."

His harsh voice pierced her soul as she tried to kick him away. But, he was too fast for her. With smooth movements, he bound her wrists to the arms of the chair and twisted a cord around her ankles.

Annie glared at him. "Let me go! Mommy!"

In response, Colleen reached around and gagged her daughter. Father Sullivan got up and slowly walked to the back of the room. He returned, swaying a metal container that hung from a long silver chain. Back and forth. Back and forth. Annie was mesmerized. Time stood still. She barely noticed the cloud of smoke circling around the priest. Her eyes were fixed on the canister as the sweet, pungent smell of incense filled the small room. Back and forth. Back and forth. Like a metronome tapping out a beat. Pulling her in. Sucking her under.

Father Sullivan stood in front of Annie, put the purple stole around his neck and began chanting the Our Father prayer in Latin. "Pater noster qui es in caelis, sanctificetur nomen tuum. Adveniat regnum tuum. Fiat voluntas tua, sicut in Caelo et in terra... "

Annie paid no attention. The incense and the chanting were making her sleepy. She dropped her head to her chest.

Yank! Father Sullivan grabbed Annie's hair and pulled her head back. An exorcism wouldn't work if the subject was asleep.

What the heck? The pain from her scalp caused Annie to regain her senses, but she pretended to sleep. She was going to fight him with every breath in her body.

Infuriated, the priest slapped her face. "Open your eyes!" He slapped her again, harder. "You will not deceive me, demon. Leave this child!"

Annie could hear her mother whimpering in the corner. After one more slap, Annie decided to take action. She tried to stand, but the straps around her wrists forced her to crouch. With the chair across her back, she swung around with all her might. The chair hit the priest right between his legs.

Umph! Pain shot through her arm as her momentum threw her to the floor, but her agony quickly turned to joy when she saw Father Sullivan writhing on the floor. *Bull's eye.*

Joy turned to fear as she watched the priest slowly get up and move toward her. His face dripped with malice as he reached for a large wooden crucifix. Annie tried to drag herself toward her mother, but the heavy chair kept her pinned in the corner. Her body tensed as she anticipated his next attack. *Think, Annie, think.* He crept closer, chanting as he advanced. His eyes narrowed as he bent down over her body, and Annie seized her opportunity. Her bound legs shot up, crushing his nose. Colleen screamed as the priest's blood covered her child.

Father Sullivan roared in pain and raised the wooden crucifix over his head. Annie froze in terror as his arm swung down. Without warning, her eyes rolled up, and she started to shake uncontrollably. The seizures caused her strapped arms to knock the chair against the wall. *Bang, bang, bang.* A death knoll.

Crash! Emir's red convertible landed in the room.

Chapter 29

Emir instantly assessed the situation, leaped out and dragged the priest away from Annie. When he fought back, Emir hit him with a right uppercut followed by a kidney punch. Father Sullivan collapsed on the floor for the second time that afternoon.

A distraught Ming knelt down beside the convulsing Annie. As Emir leaned over Annie, Colleen pulled on his arm. "Leave her. The rites are working. The devil is leaving."

He shook her off and removed Annie's gag. As blood started to trickle down the side of her mouth, he tore off his shirt and gently wiped her face. His voice was restrained as he spoke to the 911 dispatcher, but his face was dark with fury when he turned toward Colleen.

"What have you done?"

Colleen pushed him. "Saving her soul!"

Emir grabbed her arms before she could shove him again. His words came low and fast. "She's having seizures because she thought the priest was going to kill her."

Emir's anger began to frighten Colleen. "But Father John said—"

He had to control an overpowering urge to punch the wall. "I don't care what he said." He released her arms so that he could clench his fists. "It's exactly what happened after the shark attack. You know that." He glared at her and took a step forward. "You let this priest convince you something supernatural was happening."

Colleen was trembling as she stepped back. "But she hit him with the chair and broke his nose!"

Emir's voice swelled with pride as he spoke. "That wasn't the devil. That was Annie!"

The police and paramedics responded to Emir's 911 call. While the medics worked on stabilizing Annie, the police officer took statements from Father Sullivan, Colleen, Ming and Emir. Once Annie's seizures stopped, and she could speak, the police officer questioned her.

She spoke in a soft, halting voice. "He wanted to kill me."

When the medic reported that Annie had suffered a broken arm and severe psychological trauma, the officer reached for his handcuffs and approached the priest.

Father Sullivan was stunned. "What do you think you're doing?"

"Father John Sullivan, you're under arrest for assaulting a minor. You have the right to remain—"

The priest twisted away from him. "You can't arrest me. This is a religious ritual."

The officer shrugged, pulled the priest's arms behind his back and handcuffed him. "That's your attorney's problem. Right now, you're going for a ride."

The officer looked at the priest's broken nose and then looked at Emir. "You do that?"

Emir smiled and pointed at Annie. "Nope, that was all her."

Father Sullivan was out on bond in a couple of hours, but that was plenty of time for the reporters to gather in front of the police station. Microphones picked up his attorney's steady stream of "No comment" as they made their way to the waiting car.

Meanwhile, photographers were waiting as Annie, Emir and Ming left the hospital. Annie's left arm was in a sling, and her face looked bruised and battered. Colleen trailed behind, pleading with them to talk to her. Emir shepherded Annie into a taxi and left Colleen standing on the curb as the cab sped away.

When they arrived back at the house, Ming sat down at the computer to catch up on their email. "Hey, guys. We got an email from an attorney who's offering to represent you for free if you want to sue Father Sullivan for assault."

Annie plopped down on the couch and moaned. "I don't want to think about that now."

Emir and Ming rushed to her side. Ming looked forlorn. "I'm sorry, Annie. Can we get you anything?"

Annie groaned. "No, I just want to be left alone."

Annie slept until suppertime and was feeling a little better when she awoke. "Something smells good, Dr. Daphne."

Emir's mother smiled at her recuperating houseguest. "It's not my doing. Emir and Ming made dinner tonight."

Ming walked in. "We barbecued chicken for you. First time I ever cooked outdoors, but Emir's a pro."

Annie smiled. "I'll be the judge of that."

Emir carried the platter of chicken pieces in and set it on the table. "We've also got french fries and chocolate ice cream for dessert. All your favorites."

Ring, ring.

Daphne excused herself and went in the kitchen to answer her phone. "No! Absolutely not!" Mehmet looked down at his plate while Ming and Annie stared at each other. They had never heard Emir's mother raise her voice inside the house. "Not until you get professional help!"

When she returned to the table, Daphne casually mentioned that Colleen would be staying with a friend for a few days and would be by early in the morning to pick up her things. Annie nodded to indicate that she understood and finished her meal in silence.

The story made the local evening news with reporters calling for disciplinary action against the priest. When questioned, the bishop refused to comment, on the advice of Father Sullivan's attorney.

Liberal television networks picked up the early news feed and broadcast an update on their evening talk shows. Father McCarthy, the Jesuit priest in New

York who had previously defended Annie's peace movement on the show, happened to be listening.

Annie had contacted him a few weeks ago asking for suggestions on ways to combat Father Sullivan's accusations, and he had not yet gotten back to her. Tonight, he was so offended by Father Sullivan's extraordinary actions that he decided to take things one step further. He recorded the segment and sent it to the Vatican along with his background material, comments and recommendations.

Chapter 30

The next evening when Daphne was fixing dinner, the guardhouse called to say that Sophia Mendes from Child Protective Services wanted permission to come to the house. When she arrived, Daphne let her in and invited her to sit in a chair facing the couch. Annie sat between Daphne and Mehmet on the couch while Ming and Emir stood behind her. Both of them instinctively placed a protective hand on her shoulder.

"Thank you for seeing me. I'm here this evening because my Director saw the footage of Annie leaving the hospital. We've heard bits and pieces about what happened, but I need to hear it from Annie and Mrs. McDoogan in their own words."

Daphne squeezed Annie's hand and answered the social worker. "Mrs. McDoogan is staying elsewhere for a few days."

"Okay, Annie will you please tell me what happened in the rectory, particularly with regards to the role your mother played in the exorcism. With your permission, I will be recording our conversation."

Annie nodded her assent and began recalling the events of the previous day. She mentioned that her mother had been the one who gagged her. That's all she knew because the seizures started after she broke the priest's nose, and she had no memory of what happened after that.

Sophia asked her a few follow-up questions, and Annie was forced to reply that her mother had stayed back in the corner of the room as Father Sullivan slapped her. She also admitted that she never heard her mother object or ask the priest to stop the exorcism.

Sophia gave Annie a sympathetic smile. "I'm familiar with your history because I watch the news. But, for the record, please tell me why you and your mother are living here with the Polats."

Annie grimaced. "I'm here until the two men who have made repeated attacks on Ming, Emir and myself are caught and sitting in jail. They set fire to our home in Coral Springs, and when Dr. Daphne offered me and my mom a place to stay, we agreed. I think we all believe that this gated community is the safest place for us right now. We've made a lot of enemies because of our peace movement." Mehmet and Daphne both embraced this spunky young girl.

Sophia waited patiently until they released Annie. She leaned forward in her chair. "I agree that staying here is your best option if the Polats are willing to accept responsibility for you." They both nodded. "However, I will recommend that the court issue an order forbidding your mother to spend time alone with you or to spend the night in this house until she's completed a mandatory course of counseling. She can return once the psychiatrist clears her, and you agree to allow her back. Is this satisfactory?"

Annie's eyes welled up with tears of gratitude, thankful that she wouldn't have to go into foster care. "Thank you."

"No, no, no! Mommy! Help me! He's coming for me! Mommy!" Annie was covered in sweat, and her heart was racing as she waited for the priest to strike. "Mommy!"

"Annie, Annie. Wake up." Ming gently shook her terrified roommate. "You're dreaming."

Annie's wild eyes sprang open, and it took her a few moments to understand where she was. She broke down sobbing when she realized she was safe. "It was so real. He was going to kill me with the crucifix."

Ming's eyes filled with tears as she looked at her suffering friend. "You're safe here. We're all safe here. From now on, nobody leaves this house alone. There will always be at least two of us together. Okay? Nobody can beat two of us. I don't care who they are."

Annie wiped her eyes. "Okay. Can you leave the bathroom light on?"

"Sure thing. Night, Annie."

The nightmares continued all week. Sometimes the priest was the attacker, and sometimes Colleen was about to strike. One particularly disturbing dream even had a shark with a cross clutched in its jaws preparing to hit her. She wasn't eating, ached all over and couldn't focus long enough to answer her share of the emails. When she started spending most of the day alone in her room, Daphne convinced her to see Dr. Lamberti, and Emir drove her to her appointment the next afternoon.

Knock, knock.

"Come in, Annie."

Annie shuffled in, hunched over, and sat down in her usual seat. As she looked up at Dr. Lamberti, she started picking at her face. "Hello."

Oh, that poor child. "How are you feeling?"

Annie shrugged.

"Tell me about the exorcism. I saw the report on the news, but I'd like to hear it from you."

Annie shook her head. "No, no, no!"

Dr. Lamberti leaned back in her chair. "Annie, you know that none of this is your fault."

"Yes, it is." Annie spoke so softly that Dr. Lamberti had to strain to hear her.

"No, Annie. You are the victim here."

"I started the whole thing."

Dr. Lamberti leaned across her desk. "You had an out-of-body-experience when you were clinically dead that changed your life. You want to make the world a better place. That's a worthy cause and something to be proud of. New ideas are always ridiculed until they're accepted. You just have to give it time."

Annie looked at her with tears in her eyes. "Father Sullivan was going to kill me."

The psychiatrist shuttered. "Any progress on his criminal case?"

Annie sighed. "The district attorney's office called yesterday and said they aren't going to pursue it. There are too many precedents against us." She stared at the floor.

"Something about First Amendment rights for freedom of religion." A tear started rolling down her cheek. "We can't seem to win no matter what we do. It's not fair."

Dr. Lamberti frowned as she considered alternatives. "Can't you sue him in civil court?"

Annie looked up. "Yes. I have an attorney who offered to represent me for free. Because my arm is broken, he thinks the Church will eventually settle out of court."

"Well, that's good news."

Annie shrugged. "It may take years before we're offered a settlement. Meanwhile, Father John can do what he wants."

"How does your mother feel about all of this?"

Annie mumbled her reply. "Haven't seen her or talked to her."

Dr. Lamberti paused for a moment to write some notes. "How does that make you feel?"

"Miserable."

Dr. Lamberti nodded. "Maybe it's time to do something about that."

"Maybe."

The doctor leaned back in her chair. "Anything else going on you want to talk about?"

Annie sat up straighter. "They still haven't caught the two men who burned our house." She started twisting her hair around her finger. "Ming's father thinks he's seen their gray pickup following him home from his concerts." She began picking at invisible spots on her face. "He called the police, but they haven't seen anyone." Her breathing became more rapid and shallow.

Dr. Lamberti reached over and removed Annie's fingers from her face. She continued to hold her hand as she spoke. "Take a deep breath, Annie. I have an idea that may help." Annie relaxed a bit, so Dr. Lamberti continued. "You're making a lot of money from the website sales, right?"

Annie nodded with a puzzled look on her face.

"Why don't you hire an armed bodyguard to accompany him to and from the concerts?"

Annie's smile filled the room. "We can do that! Thank you."

Dr. Lamberti folded her arms and smiled. "Now, I have a few things you can do that should help you feel better." Annie looked expectantly at her doctor. "I want you to start exercising every day."

"I've got a broken arm!"

"You can still walk. Ming or Emir can go with you. If Emir has an exercise bicycle, you can start working out on that as well."

Annie made a face. She was never one that liked to exercise. "Don't frown, Annie. I want you to start doing fun things too."

"Like what?"

"You told me that your father taught you how to play chess. Maybe somebody in the house will play with you, or you can play online with people from all over the world."

"Hmmm... What else you got?"

Dr. Lamberti laughed. She was relieved to see Annie's playfulness returning. "Maybe you can start learning some Middle Eastern recipes. Emir's mother has been cooking for you for quite a while now. It would be a nice gesture."

Annie's face lit up. "Yes! That's what I'll do! I love the spices she uses. Thank you! I can plant an herb garden for her too."

Dr. Lamberti relaxed, and they talked for another half hour. She knew Annie was on the road to recovery, at least for a while. This kid was a lightning rod for danger.

Chapter 31

Annie missed her mom, but she knew things would have to change if they were ever going to reconcile. She could never again allow herself to be put in a situation where her mother would betray her. She had to give her a high-stakes ultimatum: agree or lose your daughter.

Annie invited her mother to the house for lunch and spent the morning rehearsing what she wanted to say. During the upcoming conversation with her mom, Annie would have to be the authority figure, and she wasn't sure she was entirely comfortable with that. It wasn't natural. Kids are taught to obey their parents and not the other way around. But, it was the only way.

When the doorbell rang, Annie tucked her hair behind her ears, straightened her shoulders and opened the door. For an instant, mother and daughter were frozen in time. Colleen broke the spell with an awkward smile and a kiss on the cheek. When Annie cringed at her mother's touch, Colleen walked in without speaking and sat down in the living room. Annie wanted to throw up, but she managed to sit on the couch opposite her mother's chair. Memories from the attack threatened to overwhelm her, but Annie shoved them down. "Thanks for coming, Mom." Annie's voice was ice. "I'm glad you called, honey. I've been worried about you." Colleen was trying to break through her daughter's resistance.

Annie wasn't going to let that happen. "What you did is unforgivable, but maybe we can move past it. I have important work to do, and I could use your help."

"You know I would do anything for you."

"Do anything for me?" Annie forgot her rehearsed script and slammed her good hand on the arm of the couch. "You led me into a trap! You let him slap me! You did nothing to stop him, and you didn't help me when I was having seizures!" Annie got up and walked toward her mother. "How can you sit there and not even apologize?"

Colleen stood up and held out her arms. "I thought your soul was in danger. Father John convinced me that all the signs were there, and when people started being killed... But, I'm in therapy, honey, and it's helping. I know now that I should have asked for help when dad died, but I wanted to be strong for you."

Annie grabbed her mother's purse and started rummaging through it. She found what she was looking for and triumphantly held up a small plastic container. "Here's the holy water that you started carrying around after daddy died." She twisted off the cap and poured the contents over her head. "Look! If I were possessed, I'd be growling and vomiting all over you."

She glared at her mother. "Give me your cross." Annie took the gold chain and put it over her head. "See? A devil wouldn't allow me to wear a crucifix. You're believing what he tells you because he was daddy's best friend."

Colleen hung her head. "Maybe."

Annie sighed. "I did the same thing. I kept making excuses for him because of daddy. That has to stop. He looked at me like he was going to kill me!"

Colleen gasped. "He wouldn't. He loves you."

Annie shook her fist. "You were behind him. You couldn't see his face. That's why I had the seizures. I thought he was going to hit me with that heavy crucifix!"

Colleen wrapped her arms around her baby. "I'm so sorry. Please forgive me. I'm trying to work through this."

Annie didn't answer but placed her good arm on her mother's back. The two stood there for a few minutes before Annie stepped back. "I need to stop him, and you have to help me or things will never be right between us again."

Colleen nodded. "What do you want me to do?"

A few miles away, Father Sullivan was completing the monthly accounting records for the church. The bishop may have appointed another priest to say the Sunday Mass, but Father Sullivan was still responsible for depositing the collection plate donations.

As he was entering the latest amounts in the general ledger, an idea formed in his head. He immediately discarded the thought and continued balancing the books. But, it kept coming back to him, no matter how hard he tried to ignore it.

Shaking his head, he got up and went out for a jog. He ran faster and further than usual and was sore and dehydrated when he returned an hour later. The idea was still there.

In dismay, he knelt down and said twice as many evening prayers as he normally did. When he finished, the thought still consumed him. After an hour, he had a plan.

He picked up his cellphone. "Hi, Bob. It's Father Sullivan. I've got another computer job for you if you want it." He paused for a minute. "Whatever you think is fair. You can start tomorrow. I've found the money."

Chapter 32

The kids' popularity surged after the police arrested Father Sullivan. Emir was a hero once again, and all was forgiven.

A photo of Annie wearing her mother's cross stopped the talk of satanic possession, and the teens were feeling so good that they agreed to another interview with Maddie Greenwald. Annie didn't want any more trouble and warned Emir and Ming not to let Maddie steer them into talking about religion.

As usual, Maddie arrived with her photographer, Paul. Only this time, Emir whistled when he saw her. Maddie looked like a million bucks in her fashionable resort wear, and she thanked him while Paul spent a considerable amount of time making up the girls. They were going to be on the cover of the domestic and international issues and needed to look great. The girls were giddy as Paul looked around for the best location for the shots. He finally decided on an outdoor shoot with the kids sitting in and on Emir's red convertible.

He snapped a variety of poses before leaving to catch an early flight home.

Maddie was anxious to get started and asked everybody to follow her to the living room. Since the convertible was going to be featured on the cover, she decided to begin her interview with questions about the exorcism and Emir's role in interrupting it. She took out her notepad, turned on the recorder and leaned back in her chair.

"Let's start with Emir. Tell me, why did you crash through the front of the rectory? Did you knock on the door first?"

Emir rubbed his forehead as he recalled the details of that day. "Ming and I drove up and decided to look in the windows before knocking."

Ming chimed in. "That was my idea!"

Emir ignored her interruption and continued with his story. "We saw Annie on the floor in the corner, strapped to a chair and covered with blood. Father Sullivan was walking toward her and raising a heavy-looking wooden crucifix over his head. From the back, it looked like he was getting ready to hit her." Emir clutched his hands together to keep them from shaking. "That's when Annie's seizures started, and Father Sullivan began shouting something about the devil leaving her."

Ming jumped in. "Emir was so mad. I thought he would kill the priest. He ran to the car and stomped on the gas pedal. Next thing I know, I'm looking through a hole and see Emir jumping out. I ran inside the rectory to help."

Emir frowned. "I knew I had to get the gag out of Annie's mouth. She could have choked on her own vomit or swallowed her tongue." Emir dropped his head in his hands for a moment.

Maddie encouraged him to continue. "And then what happened?"

Emir looked up with sad eyes. "I called 911. The police came, arrested the priest, and the rest of us went to the hospital."

Maddie looked toward Annie. "What was your mother doing during all of this?"

Annie shook her head. "I'm not talking about my mother."

Maddie persisted. "Wasn't she there? Did she help?"

Annie's voice got louder. "That topic is off limits."

"But did she help?"

Emir's voice was stern. "Drop it, Maddie, or the interview is over."

Maddie sighed. "Okay, anything new with the lawsuit?"

Annie calmed down. "No. My attorney says the civil case and any appeals may drag on for years. The Church has a lot of high-powered attorneys."

Maddie paused for a minute and then brought up a different subject. "How's the peace movement doing? Any updates?"

Emir answered. "The opposition is quiet now, and the majority of our emails are supportive." Emir handed Maddie a sheet of graph paper. "Here are the crime statistics for the past two months for large cities around the world. Violent crime dropped about 12 percent! It's amazing!"

Maddie nodded. "It does seem to be a good start. How do you plan to make it even more effective?"

Annie leaned forward. "We want to ask everyone to think about one of the peace images at noon every day. No matter where they live. Spend a couple of minutes, picturing a white dove, a large V or both. These are the universal symbols of peace."

Maddie was puzzled. "Why noon?"

Annie answered. "People are usually on a lunch break then, so they have the time to concentrate without distractions." She twirled her hair for a minute. "It'd be great if the schools used the PA system to announce a two-minute peace pause at noon."

Maddie wrote some notes. "Peace pause is a catchy phrase. That may help people accept it, and it's an easy slogan to remember." She paused to write herself a reminder. "Why everyone at the same time?"

Annie stood up and paced around the room, collecting her thoughts. "Research shows that telepathy is more effective when a group of people simultaneously send the same message."

Maddie nodded. "But everybody isn't in—"

Annie interrupted. "Yes, I know everybody's not in the same time zone. But, there are enough people in each zone to make it work." She shrugged. "I hope."

Ming got up, walked over and put her arm around Annie. "You never know until you try. Annie thinks science is on our side, and that's good enough for me."

Maddie wrote a bit more on her pad. "Speaking of you, have any of the movie studios or television producers contacted you about including subliminal peace messages in their movies and shows?"

Ming's face fell. "No, not a word."

Maddie shook her head. "That's too bad. I think it's a great idea. I'll include it in the article, and maybe someone's kid can persuade them to do it."

Ming smiled. "Thanks."

Maddie pointed her finger at Annie. "Anything you want to say to Father Sullivan?"

Annie nodded. "He slapped me, broke my arm and terrorized me. The district attorney won't touch him, and the bishop ignores me. I hope somebody stops him. Any way they can."

Chapter 33

Annie, Ming and Emir planned to spend a quiet weekend together. The trial was scheduled for the end of September, and they had no appearances booked until after the case was heard. They didn't want anything to happen that might prejudice a jury against Annie. There was no telling what Father Sullivan might cook up, so they decided to lay low and wait things out.

Emir wanted no more drowning incidents and insisted that Ming allow him to give her swimming lessons. She laughed and jumped at the opportunity. Spending hours in the pool with a shirtless Emir was her idea of a good time. Annie wasn't crazy about that idea and volunteered to help. They spent the morning in the pool, and Ming behaved herself and made great progress.

Annie had taken Dr. Lamberti's advice and had been exercising every day. Her slimmed-down figure looked great in her electric blue one-piece swimsuit. The gash in her thigh had completely healed, but she didn't have enough money to pay for cosmetic surgery to mask the damage. Since Ming and Emir admired her battle with the shark, she considered the scar a badge of honor when she was around them. However, she still wore long pants in public and avoided the beach. If she won the lawsuit, maybe she could use some of that money for a plastic surgeon. She sighed and went inside to make some sandwiches and iced tea as Emir demonstrated the side stroke.

Ming looked puzzled when Emir stopped swimming to watch Annie walk indoors. Suddenly, she understood. How could she have been so blind? She made up her mind to help both of her friends who had risked their lives to save hers.

"Emir, if you want to date Annie, we can double, and I promise not to leave you alone with her."

Emir's jaw dropped at the sudden announcement. "She doesn't want to date me. She and Tom text each other every day. She's always checking her phone."

Ming hit him in the arm. "Wake up! Tom's in Ohio, and you're sharing a house with her. You waiting for a written invitation?"

Emir shook his head. "No, I don't want to ruin what we've got. Just stay out of it, Ming. We're fine."

"Yeah, and I'm President of the United States."

When Annie brought lunch out, Ming decided to cause some mischief. "Hey, Annie, you want to go to the movies tonight?"

Annie shrugged. "Sure. But, how are we going to get there?"

Ming grinned. "Emir will go with us, won't you Emir? We'll even let you pick the movie since you're driving."

When they arrived at the theater, Ming went in the row first, followed by Emir and then Annie. After a couple of minutes, Ming went out to buy popcorn and had everybody slide over when she returned. Emir smiled as he sat in the darkened room. He was no longer the man in the middle.

Ring, ring.

Annie pulled the phone out of her pocket. "Hi, Mom. What's up?"

"Morning, honey. You busy? I'm going to look at a rental house and want you to see it."

"Mom, you know I can't be alone with you until your shrink gives the okay."

"That's fine. Bring Ming and Emir."

"What's the address?"

Colleen laughed. "It's across the street from you. See you in an hour." *Click.*

Sunday was turning out to be a good day for the McDoogans. Annie loved the rental house, and the owner was such a fan of theirs that she was letting them rent it dirt cheap. She had no mortgage to pay, so all Colleen had to do was to pay enough rent to cover the property tax, hazard insurance and homeowner association fees. In addition, the three-bedroom house came furnished, so Colleen didn't have to spend the insurance money from the fire on furniture. The lease would start on August 1, and Annie would be going back to her old school. Colleen's psychiatrist had told her that she would probably get a clean bill of health in a couple of weeks and could then resume her guardianship role. Annie was ecstatic, and Emir was walking around in a daze of happiness, bumping into furniture and knocking over knickknacks. Ming, however, had mixed emotions.

She was happy for her friends. But, once the attackers were caught, she would have to go back to Coral Springs. Before the fire, she and Annie had planned to take some classes together their junior year. That wouldn't happen now. Maybe she could persuade her parents to buy something here. She had enough money saved to help with the down payment, and she really would feel safer in a gated community. She had never liked the fact that her parents had chosen not to live with them at Emir's house. She tried calling her father to discuss it, but nobody picked up. She left him a message asking him to call her back. *Strange, they usually stay home on Sunday.*

Annie made Colleen lunch after they had looked in every corner of the rental, finding new little surprises in every room. Annie was glad that her mother seemed so happy. She was in intensive therapy and saw the psychiatrist every day. She had gotten back in touch with old friends and joined a bridge group at the community center. Colleen was also able to focus on her work for the first time in months and had a signed offer for a million-dollar house. Her life was back on track.

Annie hugged her mom with her good arm. "It looks like our luck is finally changing."

185

Ring, ring.

Annie picked up her cellphone. "Hello?"

"Your time will soon be here. You can't stay behind walls forever, although you're safer than those that don't." His menacing laugh raised goose bumps on Annie's arms.

"Guards can be killed. Walls can be climbed, and schools can be bombed. You'll never be safe. I will find you and take you out. But, I want it to be slow and delicious. You'll learn how to please a man before you die. You'll pay for what you've done, angel." *Click.*

Chapter 34

By suppertime, Ming still hadn't heard from her parents. She was too upset to eat and paced back and forth while the others tried to enjoy their meal. Finally, Emir couldn't take it anymore and offered to drive her by her house.

Ming was bouncing in the front seat, chewing her fingernails and urging Emir to drive faster. Annie was in the back, rubbing her shoulder, trying to calm her down.

Ming's anxiety level was escalating by the minute. "Take the Interstate. It's faster!"

Emir immediately switched over to the right lane to make the access ramp. *Screech! Hoooonk!* The smell of burning rubber filled the air as the car behind him fought to avoid a collision. It barely missed hitting the convertible as it fishtailed into the next lane. They were safe, but it left them trembling. Annie spun around and was relieved to see the other car straighten out and continue on its way.

Annie hit Emir on his back. "Are you trying to kill us?"

Ming defended him. "But we have to—"

"Shut up and let him drive, or we're not going to make it." Annie was shaken and furious, and she was in no mood to listen to excuses. "We're doing this, so you'll stop your whining, and we can have some peace. There's nothing wrong with your parents."

Ming hung her head as tears welled up in her eyes and slowly rolled down her cheeks.

They saw the yellow police tape from halfway down the street. Ming screamed and reached for her door handle, but Annie grabbed her from behind and stopped her from jumping out of the speeding car. Emir slowed down and parked in front of the smoldering ruins. The house was destroyed.

"No, no, no, no, no!" Ming didn't move as she stared transfixed at the scene.

Emir put his arm around her and pulled her close as he kissed the top of her head. "Maybe your parents got out."

Ming shuddered and shook her head. "No, they would have called."

The rest of the day was a blur. Emir called the police, who told him that the fire had been deliberately set. The neighbors reported that a gray pickup had been seen in the area during the day. Ming called her Uncle Joe in Georgia to tell him the sad news, and he told her that her parent's will specified him as her legal guardian and executor of the estate. He would fly down tomorrow, arrange the funeral service and contact their attorney. He suggested that Ming go back to the Polat's house and try to rest. He'd take care of everything for her.

Ming wasn't ready to leave. She got out, walked under the police tape and sat on her front lawn, rocking slowly, staring into the ashes. Emir was getting ready to get out of the car when Annie stopped him.

"She needs some time alone. Right now, it's barely registering. She knows we're here for her when she's ready."

Emir sighed. "It seems like your fire was a trial run. This time they got it right."

Annie frowned and got into the front seat. They were probably going to be here until it got dark. "I hope those guys fry."

The ride home was a silent one. Ming rested her head against Emir's shoulder and closed her eyes. The motion of the car was comforting as the vehicle carried her away from her childhood. She was on her own.

Emir's mother had a sedative ready for Ming, and she slept through the night. Her Uncle Joe arrived in the morning and sat in the kitchen getting to know her friends and drinking coffee with Colleen. Lilly had been telling him stories all summer about their adventures, and he was pleasantly surprised to see that their fame hadn't gone to their heads. Eventually, he and Colleen refilled their cups and carried them out to the deck to continue their chat in private as they waited for Ming to wake up.

Annie rushed to her bedroom door as soon as it opened. "I'm so sorry I said those mean things in the car. I didn't know."

"Nobody knew. I just had a feeling." Ming wiped the tears from her eyes and looked around the room.

"Uncle Joe!" Ming ran outside, landed on his lap and hugged him for a long, long minute. She finally loosened her grip so that he could speak.

"Ah, princess. This is a bad time, but we'll get through it together." His eyes filled with tears as he choked on his words. "Your parents were wonderful people." He turned her head and lifted her chin, so he could look into her eyes. "They were very proud of you."

The dam broke, and Ming cried, sitting on his lap like a young child, for 20 minutes. The wailing turned to sobs and then to sniffles. "Did they suffer?"

He shook his head. "I called the fire inspector this morning, and he told me they found them both in bed. That means that they died from smoke inhalation before the fire ever reached them. They died peacefully in their sleep." He kissed her forehead. "Don't worry about them. It's another step on their road to Enlightenment, and they're doing it together."

Ming smiled and put her head on his chest. "Thanks, Uncle Joe." They sat in silence for a few minutes. "What's the next step?"

He tightened his arms around her. "The funeral is Wednesday morning at the temple, and the bodies will be buried in the graveyard in Coral Springs." He thought for a moment. "A burial is all right with you rather than cremation?"

Ming's eyes started watering again. "Yes, there's been enough fire."

Colleen spoke for the first time. "I'll go to the mall and buy you a nice white dress for the funeral. Annie looked in your closet and didn't see anything appropriate."

Ming nodded. "Thanks. Uncle Joe... do I have to move to Georgia and live with you?" Her shoulders shook with silent sobs.

Joe and Colleen exchanged glances before Colleen reached over and put her hand on Ming's knee. "Honey, your uncle and I agreed that you can live across the street with Annie and me if you want."

Annie's shout made everybody smile. "We can be sisters!" She quickly clamped her hand over her mouth when she realized that this wasn't a happy occasion. "Sorry."

Tears were rolling down Ming's cheeks as she looked at her new family. "Thank you."

Colleen made a silent promise to the heartbroken Ming. *Father John's words are responsible for this, and I will make him pay.*

There was a large turnout for the funeral Wednesday morning. The Changs were very popular within the arts community, and some of Ming's classmates came as well. Instead of a eulogy, Ming wrote a ballad to her parents, and her voice soared over the bowed heads. I was a gut-wrenching performance, and the first time that Ming didn't care about an audience. There was no wig and no colored contact lenses. It was just Ming, singing to her parents, and it was beautiful.

Uncle Joe had arranged a reception at a nearby hotel for friends and family. Hot and cold dishes were served buffet style, and Ming mingled among the guests, thanking them for coming. It was a side of her that Annie and Emir had never seen, and a glimpse into the kind of gracious woman she would become. She wore her new-found dignity well.

Her girlfriends from school wanted to meet Emir, and he took it in stride when she escorted a group of giggling teenagers over to him. He was polite, but distracted, and kept looking across the room to where Annie stood surrounded by Ming's male classmates. Ming winked at him and went over to chaperone Annie.

Emir's parents smiled at each other as they saw the girls gather around Emir. The girls didn't stand a chance with him. They weren't Muslims.

Once the crowd thinned out, Uncle Joe pulled Ming aside for a quiet talk. "You look beautiful, princess, and you're holding up well. I'm very proud of you."

"Thank you."

"When the McDoogan's house burned, your mother sent me all the financial information and important contacts that you would need in case anything happened to them. This week, I've notified the banks and brokerage firms that you're the heir. If you're careful, you'll have enough for drama school when you graduate."

Ming nodded.

"That's enough for now. I'm leaving tomorrow, but you know how to reach me if you need me." He kissed her cheek. "I'm glad you've made such good friends. They'll help you through this."

He snapped his fingers. "One last thing. I want you to promise me that you'll see Dr. Lamberti within the next two weeks. You saw what happened to the McDoogan family. I want you to get grief counseling as soon as possible. It'll help you cope and stay strong. Promise?"

"I promise. Love you."

"Love you more."

Chapter 35

Now that Annie had started wearing a cross around her neck, Father Sullivan found himself in the awkward position of having to change tactics. The satanic possession charge didn't seem plausible anymore. However, he still believed that Annie was a threat and that more deaths would occur if she were allowed to continue her quest. He needed to stop her, and this time around, he wouldn't be acting alone.

His first step was to contact his friends at the conservative news station and arrange for an interview next week. The national exposure would do him good and help him build his team.

After that, he began to reach out to the televangelists who spoke out against Annie after the New York riot. They had been quiet lately, and he wanted to energize them. He would show the world that he was a leader of men, and someone who looked after their best interests.

Finally, he called and followed up with Bob to see how the computer hacking was going. The priest was whistling when Colleen called and invited him to lunch on Thursday.

They met at Sea Watch restaurant over on the beach and chose to eat upstairs in the less crowded lounge. The pair chatted casually as they waited for their white wine and seafood salads. Colleen was warm and engaging, and her old friend was relieved to find that she bore him no ill will for her daughter's injuries.

When the food came, Colleen checked her phone for messages and then placed her cell in the middle of the table next to the bread basket.

"So, John, how are you handling everything?"

He laughed. "I must admit that things could be better." Colleen smiled to encourage him to continue. "The bishop doesn't like all the publicity about the lawsuit and is going to ask our attorneys to speed up the trial date."

Colleen nodded. "That's probably a good idea. The kids' article is going to be published in about 10 days." Father Sullivan frowned at the news. "I wasn't there for the interview, but I'm sure that they must have discussed the exorcism."

He groaned. "That'll be more bad publicity."

Colleen took a sip of wine. "You know that she's still having nightmares."

The priest sighed. "I did what I thought was right."

Colleen patted his hand. "I know. That's why I supported you. Still do." She looked around for the waitress. "More wine?"

They ate in silence until the waitress appeared with another bottle of wine. Annie smiled as the priest took a large gulp before speaking. "Thanks for the lunch. It's been a while since I've been able to relax." He put down his glass and leaned over the table. "I have a favor to ask of you."

"Of course, John, what do you need?"

He coughed and rubbed his chin. "I'd like you to testify for me about the exorcism."

Colleen hesitated. "Well... Annie will be upset."

He nodded. "Yes, but you know I had good intentions."

Colleen took another sip of wine. "I know you meant well, and I'm happy to be a witness. I can make things right with Annie after the trial. But, how can you possibly win the lawsuit when Annie has a broken arm?"

The priest leaned back and crossed his arms. "My attorneys say I'm not responsible for that because she broke her arm when she fell on it after attacking me."

Hmmph. "But what about the nightmares? Surely, Ming will testify that Annie still wakes up screaming at night."

"My lawyers can make the case that she's prone to nightmares. She had them after her father died and after the shark attack." He knocked on the table twice for good luck and took another sip of wine.

Colleen frowned. "But those don't seem like strong enough arguments for you to win the case. Is there anything else?"

He took another sip as he thought about his answer. After a few moments, he leaned over the table. "Okay, I'll tell you, but it has to be our secret."

Colleen smiled sweetly. "Of course, John, what is it?"

He grinned like a schoolboy. "I've hired Bob Greene, one of my parishioners, to hack into the kids' computers and plant false emails."

Colleen's eyebrows shot up. "You can do that?"

The priest almost giggled. "Bob can. The letters will show that they planned this in order to get the money from a lawsuit." He fist-pumped the air. "They'll say that Annie knew what she was doing the whole time and that the nightmares are fake and just part of the scheme."

Colleen took her last bite of salad. "Brilliant. Absolutely brilliant."

Chapter 36

The response to Maddie's latest magazine article was largely positive. The readers condemned Father Sullivan for his attempted exorcism, and the Sun-Sentinel columnists had a field day criticizing their local priest. Local news broadcasts carried the story as well. It was unlikely that anyone in Annie's potential jury pool had not heard about the incident.

Annie's suggestion that schools implement a two-minute "peace pause" at noon every day generated more controversy. Opponents objected to forced prayers in public schools, but supporters pointed out that no one was asking students to pray. They were simply going to be asked to focus on a peace symbol and think about it for two minutes. Supporters pointed out that the worst it could do was to keep the students quiet and calm for a short period of time each day, and nobody would object to that.

But, the subject energized the entire debate about mind control. Annie posted her response on their blog. In her statement, she emphasized that there was nothing supernatural or weird about telepathy. Practitioners were simply using the energy in their bodies to send messages into the invisible spider web that connects all of us. She wanted to use the technique to calm people and reduce violence.

Skeptics criticized the entire idea of shared thoughts, but Annie countered that the laws of physics supported everything she said. She argued that the statistics were already showing a decrease in violent behavior, so why not give it a trial run. What could it hurt? If it didn't work, it didn't work. If it did work, it could make the world a safer place. There was nothing to lose except two minutes of time five days a week. Why not give it a try and let the local school boards decide? Who doesn't want a more peaceful society?

Ming's idea of subliminal peace messages in movies and television shows started a different type of discussion. This one centered on the legality of implanting hidden messages in public media. The concerns weren't so much about peace messages, but more about the potential for abuse by producers who had their own agenda. For example, subliminal messages in support of a political candidate were often mentioned as a possibility.

Ming posted a message that hidden political messages might already be occurring without anybody's knowledge. That statement didn't satisfy anyone, and there was a lot of discussion about passing a federal law to prevent subliminal text or images. Opponents of the law countered that free speech gave the studios and the networks the right to do it. That discussion eventually died down because no one in the industry commented on it.

Annie, Ming and Emir were both shocked and amused by some of the suggestions that they received on how to stop Father Sullivan. They ranged from the direct (kill him) to the bizarre (cut out his tongue) to the morbidly funny (feed him to the gators... one chunk at a time.) Annie was disturbed that the main advice was to do away with the priest, and she quickly regretted her harsh words.

The cover photo was dynamite. Kids all over the world tore off the cover and hung it on their bedroom walls. The crusading trio were almost universally loved and admired. Almost.

Dynamite's a dangerous thing and can detonate if you're not careful. Emir's expensive red convertible was the catalyst for an explosion of jealousy and ill will. His car cost more than many families earned in a year, and in some cases, more than they would ever earn.

Emir was initially surprised at the hostility but was eventually ashamed that he hadn't considered that possibility. Maybe he was just a spoiled rich kid. That afternoon he went to a dealer and traded his beautiful red baby for a much older green sedan. He pocketed the difference and went home feeling free. He took a picture and posted it on the website with his apologies.

Daphne walked in and put a bag of groceries down on the kitchen counter. "Emir, whose car is that in the driveway?"

He answered as he was getting dressed for a tennis game. "Mine. You like it?"

Daphne went into his room. "Is that a joke? Where's the car we bought you?"

His nerves were on edge after the deaths of Ming's parents, and his mother's tone was rubbing him raw. "I traded it in. It was sending the wrong message to the kids we need to help us."

"Take it back. You can't park that thing in the driveway."

Emir put his hands on his hips and pushed out his chest. "Then, I'll use the garage, and you can park in the driveway."

Daphne took a step forward and spoke in a threatening voice. "You'll do as I say."

Emir gave her a steely stare. "I'm a man, and you can't force me to do what you want." His pent-up emotions suddenly flooded out. "I will live my life the way *I* want, and I'll not be manipulated by presents or the promise of money. I'll make my own way, and if I prefer an old car, that's what I'll get."

Daphne was surprised. He had never spoken to her like that. "You will live by our rules, go to medical school and marry a good Muslim woman."

Emir slammed his fist down on his dresser. "Didn't my suicide attempt show you anything?"

Daphne was shocked and started to stutter. "What... what... "

Emir was furious and frustrated. "Nobody ever said anything, and nothing changed, even after Father Sullivan outed me, and I started seeing Dr. Lamberti. You and dad never said anything because I embarrassed you, and now all your patients know that your son tried to kill himself. Well, now they're also going to know that I'm driving an old car. Deal with it!"

Daphne slowly sat down on his bed. "Emir—"

He turned to face her. "I don't want to hear it! You and dad push and push and push. I can't take it anymore. I may not go to medical school, and I may decide to marry a Catholic girl or a Buddhist or a Jew or an atheist or not marry anybody. It's my choice! Not yours and not dad's. Mine! And that's the way it's going to be."

Annie and Ming were watching television in the family room and heard the whole argument. When it was over, they high-fived each other, glad that Emir had finally become his own man.

Father Sullivan directed his television interview Friday night at the people who weren't enamored with the kids. His goal was to build a team of vocal community leaders who would join him in stopping Annie's activities. He spoke at length about the dangers of mind control and the loss of free will. He said that her tactics were dangerous for society.

Once he was done, the show invited viewers to call in with questions or comments for the priest. The station screened the calls to eliminate people who were angry with him about the exorcism.

Many of the callers said the voices inside their head were warning them not to let anybody mess with their mind. They were adamant that Annie should be stopped.

The most satisfying callers were from the southern Bible belt. These were the people that were most like him. They tended to be vocal and uncompromising in their beliefs, and the idea of someone interfering with their free will resonated with them.

The priest was disappointed that none of the prominent televangelists called in. It was great that the common folks were responding, but he wanted to reach the movers and shakers. He needed to lead prominent people if he was going to make a name for himself and have an effect.

The last call of the evening sent chills down Father Sullivan's spine.

"Hello, Father. This is Billy Joe from Fort Lauderdale. I'm calling to tell you that your troubles will soon be over. Little Miss Annie won't be causing you no more problems. I'll take care of everything. Just you wait and see. Yes, sir. Miss Annie will get what's coming to her."

Chapter 37

Colleen was truly happy for the first time in months. She had moved into the rental home across the street from Emir, and the psychiatrist had agreed that she could resume her parental duties. Emir had helped Annie and Ming move in yesterday, and it felt good to be settled again. The day was bright and sunny as she drove Annie, Emir and Ming to the courthouse. An opening had appeared on the judge's calendar, and he agreed to move up Annie's lawsuit. Annie was a nervous wreck, but she was glad that her case was being heard so quickly.

The reporters and photographers swarmed around them as they approached the entrance. The kids linked arms and pushed forward. Colleen followed behind saying, "No comment" as they proceeded into the courthouse and past the guards. Annie's attorney, Levi Silverman, met them in the lobby and escorted them into the appropriate courtroom. He was a short, bald man with a serious demeanor. His suit was acceptable but inexpensive, and his stooped posture made him appear much older than his actual years.

Father Sullivan and his three attorneys were already present and seated at the defendant's table. Annie and her attorney sat at the plaintiff's table. Local reporters sat on the benches behind them. They were easily identifiable in a room filled with the teenagers who were there to support Annie. Everyone stood as the judge entered from his chambers.

The plaintiff's side was the first to present their opening statement. Mr. Silverman stood and faced the jury. "Ladies and gentlemen of the jury, today I will present evidence that the defendant, Father John Sullivan, did knowingly and willfully cause bodily and psychological trauma to the plaintiff, Miss Annie McDoogan." He picked up several packets from the table and waved them in the air. "You will see X-rays and photographs of the physical injuries Miss McDoogan suffered while in the presence of Father Sullivan, and you will hear from her psychiatrist about the emotional trauma that she is still experiencing."

He stepped away from the table and spread his arms wide. "Ladies and gentlemen, you should know that Miss McDoogan will not be testifying due to the post-traumatic stress she is experiencing as a result of being terrorized by the defendant."

He walked over in front of Annie and pointed at her cast. She looked sad and in pain. "You need to decide whether or not the priest is liable for the physical and emotional damage that resulted from his actions."

The young spectators cheered as Annie's attorney sat down. The judge banged his gavel to silence them.

"Order in the court! I will not allow any disturbances to interfere with this hearing."

Annie squeezed Levi's arm, and they both waited expectantly to hear the opening remarks from Father Sullivan's lead attorney, Francis Mancini.

The Church's attorney was a tall, imposing figure as he walked over to the jury box. His magnificent head of snow-white curly hair, Roman nose and large frame oozed success and competence. Mr. Mancini's every movement showed the world that he was a winner. The jury women couldn't take their eyes off him.

"Your Honor, and valued members of the jury, we intend to prove that the plaintiff's injuries were self-inflicted and part of a devious scheme to trap the defendant for the sole purpose of collecting a monetary judgment."

The judge slammed his gavel as the court erupted in protests. "Order in the court! Order in the court! I will not warn you again."

The attorney pointed at his client. "This priest is a pillar of his community, and he is the victim here. Our evidence will leave no doubt in your mind as to his innocence."

Mr. Mancini spoke directly to the jury. "Your only duty is to decide if the plaintiff proved its case. If you have any reasonable doubts, you must find him not guilty."

After Mr. Mancini sat down, the judge addressed Annie's attorney. "Mr. Silverman, call your first witness."

"We call Dr. Leonard Morgan."

Once Dr. Morgan was sworn in and stated his credentials as a licensed emergency-room physician, he confirmed that the X-rays and photographs of Annie's bruised face were taken in the emergency room immediately after leaving the rectory. The film and photographs were presented to the jury for review.

"Mr. Mancini, do you wish to cross-exam this witness?"

"Yes, your Honor. Dr. Morgan, can you tell if the broken bone resulted from a strike, twisting or a fall?"

The doctor nodded. "Yes, the pattern of the break definitely indicates that it resulted from a fall."

"Thank you, and can you tell the court if the facial bruises could also be self-inflicted?"

Dr. Morgan frowned as he considered this possibility. "Yes, but I—"

"Thank you, Dr. Morgan, but a yes or no answer is all that's required. We have no more questions for this witness, your Honor."

"You may step down, Dr. Morgan. Mr. Silverman, call your next witness."

"We call Dr. Lisa Lamberti."

The psychiatrist was sworn in and testified that, in her opinion, Annie was suffering from a post-traumatic stress disorder as a result of the exorcism. She described the symptoms and explained that the disorder could last for the rest of Annie's life.

"Do you wish to cross-exam, Mr. Mancini?"

"No questions, your Honor."

Annie's attorney stood up. "The plaintiff rests."

"Very well. Mr. Mancini, call your first witness."

"The defense calls Colleen McDoogan."

Gasps were heard throughout the courtroom as Colleen was sworn in and affirmed that she was Annie's mother. *Her mother was testifying for the priest?* "Mrs. McDoogan, isn't it true that your daughter has a history of nightmares and depression?" Colleen nodded in agreement. "Yes. As you might expect, she was traumatized by her father's murder and her shark attack."

"So, having nightmares is not a new experience for her?"

"No."

Mr. Mancini walked up to the witness box. "Please tell the court where you were standing during the exorcism."

"I was against the wall behind Father Sullivan."

"Could you see his face or your daughter?"

"No. During much of the ritual, his back blocked her from my view."

"Did you see the defendant slap your daughter?"

"No."

"Did you see the defendant break your daughter's arm?"

"No."

"Did you see your daughter fall?"

"Yes. She was strapped to a chair and stood up to use her torso to swing the chair around and strike Father Sullivan. The momentum of her swing carried her to the floor. She landed on her side and broke her arm."

"Father Sullivan didn't push her or strike her after she attacked him?"

"No."

"We have no further questions for Mrs. McDoogan, your Honor."

"Mr. Silverman, do you wish to cross-exam?"

"Yes, your Honor. Mrs. McDoogan, in your opinion, what caused Annie to attack the defendant?"

"I suppose she was angry about being tied down, gagged and slapped."

The courtroom erupted in laughter, and the judge frowned to keep himself from smiling.

Mr. Silverman walked over to the witness chair. "You testified earlier that you didn't see the defendant slap your daughter. How do you know it occurred?"

"I could hear it, and I saw his arm swing out as if he wanted to gain speed before slapping her."

Mr. Mancini jumped up. "Objection, your Honor! The witness cannot possibly speculate as to the defendant's motives."

"Objection sustained. The jury is instructed to ignore the last comment from the witness. Continue, Mr. Silverman."

"How many times did the defendant slap Annie?"

"Three."

"I realize you couldn't see his face, but did he sound angry?"

"Yes."

"Very angry?"

"Yes."

"Thank you. We have no more questions for this witness."

"Mrs. McDoogan, you may step down. Mr. Mancini, call your next witness." Annie turned her head away from the judge and winked at her mother as she walked past.

"The defense calls Father John Sullivan."

There was a buzz in the courtroom as the priest took the stand and was sworn in. "Father Sullivan, you told your attorneys that you suspected Annie's reactions during the exorcism were premeditated. Is that correct?"

"Yes. I don't believe any 16-year-old girl is capable of inflicting such pain without rehearsing possible attack moves."

"What type of pain?"

"I was hit in the groin with a chair, and my nose was broken when she kicked it even though her ankles were bound together."

There was a rumbling of approval in the courtroom, and Annie turned and smiled at her supporters.

"In order to prove this theory, you requested your attorneys to obtain a subpoena to examine her personal computer. Is that correct?"

"Yes."

"Please tell the court what was discovered."

"An examination of her emails clearly shows that the entire scenario was planned and rehearsed."

"For what purpose?"

"To obtain a monetary judgment from the court or to induce the Catholic Church to settle out of court for a large sum of money."

"Please read the selected emails."

Father Sullivan read the emails for the next 10 minutes. "Thank you, Father. No further questions."

"Mr. Silverman, do you have any questions for this witness?"

"Yes, your Honor. Father Sullivan, please clarify one point. What led you to suspect that the plaintiff's reactions were part of a plan to deceive this court?"

"No girl her age is capable of reacting in such a manner without rehearsal."

"I believe you're incorrect in that assumption, and I accuse you of planting the damaging emails on her computer."

Mr. Mancini was on his feet. "Objection! Mr. Silverman has demonstrated no supporting evidence for such an outrageous charge!"

Levi Silverman smiled for the first time that morning. "Your Honor, I have in my possession a taped conversation between Father Sullivan and Colleen McDoogan in which he discusses his scheme to plant the emails."

Mr. Mancini's composure cracked, and beads of sweat glistened under the overhead lights. "Objection! Secretly recorded conversations are a violation of Florida's wiretapping law and cannot be submitted as evidence!"

"Your Honor, the conversation was recorded by Mrs. McDoogan on her cellphone in a public restaurant during a busy lunchtime service. There can be no presumption of privacy in this case."

"Very well. I'll allow the conversation to be heard."

The defense attorney's face was a deep red. "Objection!"

"Take it up in appeals court, Counselor. Mr. Silverman, you may play the recording."

It took the jury 30 minutes to return a guilty verdict and a recommendation that the court award Annie the entire $500,000 requested judgment. The judge increased that amount to $1,000,000.

Annie wanted a few minutes alone as she read the tweets and emails on her cellphone. Ming and Emir were back on the courthouse steps signing autographs, and Colleen and Levi were talking to the press. Annie's head was down as she focused on her phone while she walked toward the car.

She didn't see the gray pickup truck barreling toward her, but Father Sullivan did. Without a second thought, he jumped in front of the truck and pushed her out of the way.

The priest's broken body landed in the grass 20 feet away. The truck crashed into a cement wall and immediately burst into flames, incinerating the two occupants.

Chapter 38

The bishop folded his arms across his chest as he looked down at a battered Father Sullivan lying in his hospital bed. His right leg was in traction. His left arm was in a cast, and he had a collar around his neck to immobilize his head. He was expected to remain in the hospital for another month and eventually have a full recovery.

"John, I wanted to let you know that the police identified the men who hit you. It turns out that they're the same ones who started the fire at the McDoogans."

"Good." He didn't feel like saying more because he knew the bishop was here to reprimand him for lying under oath, falsifying evidence and using church money to pay for illegal activity.

The bishop continued the conversation. "I've spoken to the district attorney, and he agreed not to press charges for the perjury and computer hacking as long as we transfer you out of his jurisdiction."

"That's good." He was waiting for the ax to fall.

The bishop leaned over the bed to look him straight in the eye. "At one point, the pope was considering excommunicating you for your unnecessary exorcism. He thought it sounded more like a vendetta." The bishop waited a few minutes to let the possibility sink in.

Father Sullivan closed his eyes and waited, trying to control his ragged breathing and racing pulse. He might just have a heart attack now and save everybody a lot of trouble.

The bishop took no pleasure in watching the other man's distress. "I'm not sure how the Holy Father heard about the exorcism, but the only reason you're still a priest is because you saved that girl's life."

Father Sullivan groaned again. Maybe there was hope after all.

The bishop stood up and crossed his arms. He paused for a moment. "After much consideration and hours of prayer, I've decided to send you to Juneau."

Relief flooded the priest's bruised face. "Thank you, your Excellency, for allowing me to stay in Florida. Juno Beach is more than I deserve."

"You're right. It is. However, I'm afraid you misunderstood me. I'm sending you to Juneau, Alaska."

The big day arrived. The pope was touring the U.S. and had requested a private meeting with Annie during his Miami visit. Her stomach was full of butterflies as she dressed in her best clothes. Why did he want to see her? Was he going to criticize her for suing a priest?

Maybe he was going to excommunicate her. She was ready to go three hours early.

"Your Holiness." Annie was in awe as she knelt at the foot of his white robe to kiss his ring and receive his papal blessing. Nothing in her life compared to this moment. She was completely flustered as he took her good arm and helped her up.

"Annie, I'm glad you could meet with me. I have a few things to share with you." His slightly accented voice was authoritative.

Oh, no. Here it comes. "Yes?"

"First, I want to tell you that the Church will not be appealing your lawsuit against Father Sullivan. You will receive the check for one million dollars in two weeks."

I didn't expect that. "Thank you, your Holiness."

He smiled kindly at his nervous visitor. "Every day, I try to change the world just a little. But, I'm an old man and running out of time."

Annie shook her head and started to protest, but stopped when he held up his hand. "You're young and have a whole lifetime ahead of you. I believe you're remarkable and have the courage and determination to make the world a better place. You are a warrior who won't be stopped."

Annie's eyes filled with tears, and she began to tremble. She whispered, "Thank you."

"I've known Father McCarthy for many years, and we share some common interests. He's a very strong supporter of yours, and he is the one who made me aware of your movement and the problems with your parish priest. If you need an advisor in the future, he would be a good choice." He shook his head at the injustice this poor girl had endured. "I agree with your view of the interconnectedness among people. Starting next month all Catholic schools around the world will implement a two-minute peace pause at noon every school day."

Annie was speechless but felt like cheering and hugging the pope. "We will print cards with a white dove flying across a gold V. This will become the Vatican's new symbol of peace. Every student will receive a card to help them concentrate."

The pope put his hand on Annie's shoulder. "I hope the public schools follow our example. It's good to teach children that they can make a positive difference in this world."

He rubbed his chin before continuing. "The next thing that I tell you will have to remain a secret."

Annie's eyes were wide as saucers as she stared in amazement at the man standing in front of her. Was the pope going to tell *her* a secret?

"The Vatican has reached out to the heads of movie studios and television networks around the world. After much persuasion, many of them have agreed to include subliminal peace messages in their movies and television shows."

Annie began to jump up and down. "Ming will be thrilled! It was her idea!"

He shook his head. "No, Annie, you can't tell anyone. They don't want to take a chance that publicity-seeking politicians will introduce legislation to stop it."

Annie frowned, but his next words comforted her. "You have a silent army of very influential people supporting you, but they must remain hidden."

Annie bowed her head. "Yes, your Holiness."

After one year, the Vatican reported that areas near Catholic schools experienced a 20 percent drop in violent crime. That was sufficient incentive for many public school administrators to implement the two-minute peace pause in their classrooms. As crime continued to decrease, the heads of movie studios and television networks worked behind the scenes to spread the word. They reached out to large software companies and video game developers and suggested that they incorporate subliminal peace messages in their software applications, operating systems and Internet search engines.

After a few years, the world was inundated with hidden peace messages. Crime fell by 50 percent. Leaders directed their energy toward creating jobs and promoting the value of education. Prosperity reigned. The War on Terror was over, and the Golden Age of Peace had begun.

*****

If you enjoyed this book, please take a moment to review it on your favorite retailer's website. You can reach the author at poconnor.author@gmail.com and at pat-oconnor.com.